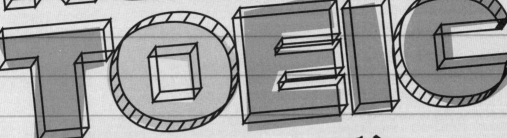

New TOEIC
漸進式
模擬試題本

作者 大賀理惠、Bill Benfield、Ann Gleason、Terry Browning

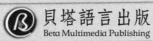
貝塔語言出版
Beta Multimedia Publishing

IRT 語言測驗中心
Language Testing Center

Pre Test

100 題

LISTENING TEST（p. 4-12）
READING TEST　（p. 13-28）把計時器設定為 38 分鐘。

LISTENING TEST 的 ◎ mp3 音軌從 Track 02 開始播放。

LISTENING TEST

In the Listening test, you will be asked to demonstrate how well you understand spoken English. The entire Listening test will last approximately 22 minutes. There are four parts, and directions are given for each part. You must mark your answers on the separate answer sheet. Do not write your answers in your test book.

Part 1

Directions: For each question in this part, you will hear four statements about a picture in your test book. When you hear the statements, you must select the one statement that best describes what you see in the picture. Then find the number of the question on your answer sheet and mark your answer. The statements will not be printed in your test book and will be spoken only one time.

Example   Sample Answer
                                                                                       Ⓐ Ⓑ ● Ⓓ

Statement (C), "They're standing near the table," is the best description of the picture, so you should select answer (C) and mark it on your answer sheet.

1.

2.

➡ *GO ON TO THE NEXT PAGE.*

3.

4.

5.

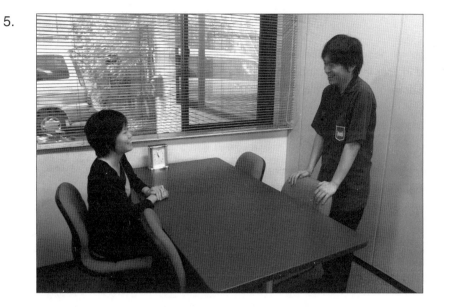

➡ *GO ON TO THE NEXT PAGE.*

Part 2

Directions: You will hear a question or statement and three responses spoken in English. They will not be printed in your test book and will be spoken only one time. Select the best response to the question or statement and mark the letter (A), (B), or (C) on your answer sheet.

Example

Sample Answer

Ⓐ ● Ⓒ

You will hear: Where is the meeting room?
You will also hear: (A) To meet the new director.
               (B) It's the first room on the right.
               (C) Yes, at two o'clock.

The best response to the question "Where is the meeting room?" is choice (B), "It's the first room on the right," so (B) is the correct answer. You should mark answer (B) on your answer sheet.

6. Mark your answer on your answer sheet.

7. Mark your answer on your answer sheet.

8. Mark your answer on your answer sheet.

9. Mark your answer on your answer sheet.

10. Mark your answer on your answer sheet.

11. Mark your answer on your answer sheet.

12. Mark your answer on your answer sheet.

13. Mark your answer on your answer sheet.

14. Mark your answer on your answer sheet.

15. Mark your answer on your answer sheet.

16. Mark your answer on your answer sheet.

17. Mark your answer on your answer sheet.

18. Mark your answer on your answer sheet.

19. Mark your answer on your answer sheet.

20. Mark your answer on your answer sheet.

Part 3

Directions: You will hear some conversations between two people. You will be asked to answer three questions about what the speakers say in each conversation. Select the best response to each question and mark the letter (A), (B), (C), or (D) on your answer sheet. The conversations will not be printed in your test book and will be spoken only one time.

21. What does Marcy do?
    (A) She's a police officer.
    (B) She's a tour guide.
    (C) She's a mechanic.
    (D) She's a tourist.

22. How long will it take Rick to drive to where Marcy is?
    (A) 2 minutes
    (B) 15 minutes
    (C) 50 minutes
    (D) 95 minutes

23. Who will probably change the flat tire?
    (A) Marcy.
    (B) One of the passengers.
    (C) Rick.
    (D) A police officer.

24. What was wrong with the presentation?
    (A) It was too short.
    (B) It wasn't well-packaged.
    (C) There were no product samples.
    (D) Some of the samples were defective.

25. What did Mr. Meyers tell Sarah?
    (A) He told her not to make any changes.
    (B) He told her not to bring samples to the presentation.
    (C) He told her to modify the presentation.
    (D) He told her that packaging wasn't the most important thing.

26. What is true about the conversation?
    (A) The man said the presentation was perfect.
    (B) The man and the woman agreed.
    (C) The man and the woman disagreed.
    (D) The woman asked the man to help her.

27. Who are the two speakers?
    (A) A cabin attendant and a passenger
    (B) A customs officer and a traveler
    (C) A gift shop owner and a customer
    (D) An airline agent and a customer

28. What does the man want?
    (A) To leave earlier than scheduled
    (B) To cancel his flight
    (C) To check in his luggage
    (D) To pay cash for his ticket

29. What time is it now, most likely?
    (A) 2:30 p.m.
    (B) 2:45 p.m.
    (C) 3:00 p.m.
    (D) 3:30 p.m.

➡ GO ON TO THE NEXT PAGE.

Pre Test

Half Test 1

Half Test 2

Full Test

30. What was the purpose of the call?
    (A) To complain
    (B) To get help
    (C) To buy something
    (D) To report an incident

31. Which department did John probably call?
    (A) Marketing
    (B) Accounting
    (C) Technical Support
    (D) Quality Control

32. How does the caller feel?
    (A) He's frustrated.
    (B) He's hungry.
    (C) He's embarrassed.
    (D) He's tired.

---

33. What is the woman complaining about?
    (A) She hasn't received her refund yet.
    (B) She hasn't canceled her subscription.
    (C) She is disappointed with the contents of the magazine.
    (D) She thinks the magazine subscription is too expensive.

34. When did the woman get her last issue?
    (A) Three months ago
    (B) Yesterday
    (C) Today
    (D) Last year

35. What will probably happen after this?
    (A) The company will go bankrupt.
    (B) The woman will continue to subscribe to the magazine.
    (C) The magazines will continue to come for 3 months.
    (D) The woman will receive her refund.

Part 4

Directions: You will hear some talks given by a single speaker. You will be asked to answer three questions about what the speaker says in each talk. Select the best response to each question and mark the letter (A), (B), (C), or (D) on your answer sheet. The talks will not be printed in your test book and will be spoken only one time.

36. Where is the library located?
    (A) The main branch
    (B) The state and federal building
    (C) Next to the book store
    (D) On East Main Street

37. What hours is the library open on Fridays?
    (A) From10 in the morning until 9 in the evening
    (B) From 9 in the morning until 9 in the evening
    (C) From 10 in the morning until 8 in the evening
    (D) From 12 noon until 8 in the evening

38. What will happen in July?
    (A) The library will be renewed.
    (B) All the library personnel will go on vacation.
    (C) The library will be relocated.
    (D) The library will be open every day.

39. What kind of weather is predicted for tonight?
    (A) Clear skies
    (B) Storm
    (C) Rain
    (D) Clouds

40. What happened on Tuesday?
    (A) The rain finally stopped.
    (B) There was a storm.
    (C) It snowed a lot.
    (D) It was a very hot day.

41. When will it be sunny again?
    (A) This morning
    (B) Tuesday afternoon
    (C) Tomorrow morning
    (D) Tomorrow afternoon

42. What is this news about?
    (A) A man went hiking and hasn't come home yet.
    (B) A helicopter crashed in the mountains, and the pilot is missing.
    (C) Police are looking for a man who killed his wife.
    (D) A dangerous criminal has escaped from jail.

43. How old is Frank Dobbs?
    (A) 20
    (B) 40
    (C) 52
    (D) 80

44. What did Frank Dobbs take with him?
    (A) A gun and a cell phone
    (B) A cell phone and a map
    (C) A map and drinking water
    (D) Drinking water and food

➡ GO ON TO THE NEXT PAGE.

Pre Test

Half Test 1

Half Test 2

Full Test

45. What kind of business is being advertised?
(A) A car dealer
(B) A discount store
(C) An electronics store
(D) A supermarket

46. How can you qualify for a discount?
(A) By going to the shopping mall and picking up a coupon
(B) By going to Richard's any time
(C) By attending the demonstration this afternoon
(D) By telling Richard you heard the ad on the Morning Show

47. How long is this special offer good for?
(A) Until all the goods have been sold
(B) Until closing time today
(C) Tomorrow at 6 p.m.
(D) For one week starting today

48. What will happen to the refrigerator during the holidays?
(A) It will be replaced with a new one.
(B) It will be repaired.
(C) It will be moved to another floor.
(D) It will be donated to charity.

49. What are employees asked to do?
(A) Eat lunch at home on Fridays.
(B) Throw away any food left in the lunch room.
(C) Remove their food from the refrigerator.
(D) Clean up their own mess at the end of each day.

50. What happened last year?
(A) The freezer broke down and had to be fixed.
(B) A box of food was left in the lunch room.
(C) Someone forgot to take their ice cream home before the holidays.
(D) There was a Christmas party, and nobody cleaned up.

This is the end of the Listening test. Turn to Part 5 in your test book.

READING TEST

In the Reading test, you will read a variety of texts and answer several different types of reading comprehension questions. The entire Reading test will last 37 minutes. There are three parts, and directions are given for each part. You are encouraged to answer as many questions as possible within the time allowed.

You must mark your answers on the separate answer sheet. Do not write your answers in your test book.

Part 5

Directions: A word or phrase is missing in each of the sentences below. Four answer choices are given below each sentence. Select the best answer to complete the sentence. Then mark the letter (A), (B), (C), or (D) on your answer sheet.

Pre Test
Half Test 1
Half Test 2
Full Test

51. The new desktop model is the most ------- computer I have ever used. I can't do without it.
    (A) reliable
    (B) reliability
    (C) relying
    (D) relied

52. Frank is a mail clerk, so his ------- is to sort out and deliver the mail to each department every morning.
    (A) behavior
    (B) action
    (C) responsibility
    (D) hobby

53. In order to promote our sales in agricultural produce, we will ------- Bill Rush and his staff attend the Farmers' Convention in Atlanta this year.
    (A) let
    (B) have
    (C) make
    (D) tell

54. Our financial advisor was so reliable that she ------- exactly when the stock market would begin to pick up and when it would fall.
    (A) will know
    (B) has known
    (C) knows
    (D) knew

55. After snatching a bag from an elderly woman, the criminal ran into a police officer and ------- right away.
    (A) caught
    (B) got caught
    (C) will catch
    (D) catchy

56. For the barbecue next Saturday, I'll bring beef and chicken, so you ------- buy them.
    (A) have to
    (B) don't have to
    (C) must
    (D) mustn't

➡ GO ON TO THE NEXT PAGE.

57. The building was burning so fiercely that there was ------- the firefighters could do to save it.
    (A) little
    (B) a little
    (C) few
    (D) a few

58. As ------- as I know, the order was shipped out the day before yesterday, and was scheduled to arrive at the client company this morning.
    (A) well
    (B) little
    (C) many
    (D) far

59. Our business this year has dropped so drastically that we will have to let ------- Fred or Nelly go.
    (A) either
    (B) neither
    (C) both
    (D) that

60. I'm all for Norman to be elected class monitor. ------- busy he was, Norman always treated us warmly and gave us lots of constructive advice.
    (A) How
    (B) How much
    (C) No matter how
    (D) Whenever

61. Samantha will be going to Beijing next week and plans to visit the Great Wall ------- she stays there.
    (A) where
    (B) during
    (C) as
    (D) while

62. ------- everyone's surprise, Tim, who was considered the shyest person in class, won first prize in the speech contest.
    (A) By
    (B) To
    (C) On
    (D) For

63. Although Joe has been working in the factory for only two weeks, he is already getting used to ------- heavy machinery.
    (A) handle
    (B) handling
    (C) have handled
    (D) handled

64. Mary-Ann has been working night shifts at a convenience store, so her husband ------- sees her.
    (A) not always
    (B) not often
    (C) hardly ever
    (D) almost

65. I suggest we hire Omega Works Studio for our next TV commercial because they will probably come up with ------- innovative design than any other company.
    (A) more
    (B) some
    (C) the most
    (D) the only

66. The company manufactures hybrid cars ------- gas consumption is 30% lower than gas-powered cars.
    (A) that
    (B) whose
    (C) what
    (D) why

67. ------- do you think I could have your
answer to my application for the housing
loan?
(A) Who
(B) Which
(C) When
(D) What

68. If ------- you, I wouldn't buy that
condominium right now. The real estate
market is booming and the prices are the
highest they have ever been.
(A) I were
(B) I am
(C) I could be
(D) I might be

69. We'll have to ------- do with oil and vinegar
for the potato salad since we are all out of
mayonnaise.
(A) work
(B) have
(C) take
(D) make

70. As a door-to-door sales representative,
Stella ------- on over 200 homes every day
selling Devon cosmetics.
(A) calls
(B) gives
(C) picks
(D) visits

➡ *GO ON TO THE NEXT PAGE.*

Part 6

Directions: Read the texts that follow. A word or phrase is missing in some of the sentences. Four answer choices are given below each of the sentences. Select the best answer to complete the text. Then mark the letter (A), (B), (C), or (D) on your answer sheet.

Questions 71-73 refer to the following advertisement.

CHARITY CONCERT

For all lovers of classical music, we are ------- to announce that an extra concert by the

71. (A) please
(B) pleased
(C) pleasant
(D) pleasing

world-famous Santa Rosa Symphony Orchestra has been added to the performance schedule at Hatfield Hall. The concert will be given on Tuesday, May 14 at 7:30 p.m. It will be a charity concert, therefore, all proceeds will be ------- to The National Childhood Cancer Foundation.

72. (A) charged
(B) paid
(C) donated
(D) distributed

This extra performance will feature the orchestra's founder and previous conductor, Frederick Charles. Mr. Charles retired last year; -------, he will return to conduct just this one performance. For the

73. (A) Although
(B) On the contrary
(C) However
(D) Consequently

program, he has selected his favorite pieces by Mozart, Beethoven and Debussy. Tickets are $50, $80 and $100, and are available directly from Hatfield Hall. For reservations, please call 1-800-888-8811, or visit our website, www.hatfieldhall.org, where you can make reservations online.

Questions 74-76 refer to the following letter.

GHG Trading
Koningslaan 35, Rotterdam, Netherlands
Phone (31) 437-8760; fax (31) 437-8761
E-mail info@ghg.co.ne

Mr. Kevin Foyle
CEO
Brabant Industries
468 Solent Avenue
Des Moines, IA 50301
USA

March 22, 2008

Dear Mr. Foyle,

Thank you for agreeing to hire GHG Trading as your sales agent for the Netherlands and Belgium. We were very impressed by your products. As you suggested, we also spoke to some of your other sales agents, and they all ------- you very highly as a business partner.

74. (A) recommend
    (B) complain
    (C) criticize
    (D) speak

First, we would like to introduce some of the latest products of yours to potential buyers at a trade show that will be ------- place in Rotterdam from October 23 to 26 this year. It will give

75. (A) holding
    (B) having
    (C) doing
    (D) taking

us the chance to demonstrate your products to people from many different countries. -------, we would like to introduce your products at other trade shows all over Western Europe.

76. (A) Consequently
    (B) Subsequently
    (C) On the other hand
    (D) On the contrary

For your information, I have enclosed a brochure giving full details of the show.
I look forward to hearing from you soon.

Sincerely,

Piet van Doorn
Sales Manager

GO ON TO THE NEXT PAGE.

Directions: In this part you will read a selection of texts, such as magazine and newspaper articles, letters, and advertisements. Each text is followed by several questions. Select the best answer for each question and mark the letter (A), (B), (C), or (D) on your answer sheet.

Questions 77-78 refer to the following advertisement.

NEW SUPERSAVER MARKET—GRAND OPENING ON SATURDAY, JULY 18

SuperSaver is pleased to announce the opening of its newest and most modern supermarket in Watsonville on Saturday, July 18, 2008. A ribbon-cutting ceremony will be held in the parking lot at 8:15 a.m., and the new store will be open for business at 9:00 a.m. Starting Sunday, the new supermarket will be open every day from 6:00 a.m. to 11:00 p.m.

In celebration of the grand opening, SuperSaver will make a donation to the Watsonville Branch Library for their Children's Reading Program and to the Watsonville High School Marching Band, who will also perform at the ribbon-cutting ceremony.

Among the departments at the new 4,000-square-meter SuperSaver supermarket will be a Meat Department offering a selection of the finest US Choice beef, and a Fresh Seafood Department. Our famous SuperSaver Deli offers a complete selection of fresh salads and a wide variety of domestic and imported cheeses. And be sure to stop by meals-to-go including SuperSaver's famous Southern Fried Chicken.

And if you need a break from shopping, find a table in the Deli snack bar and sit down to enjoy some hot soup, fresh salad, delicious sandwiches, soda, or fresh-brewed coffee.

So why not bring the family to enjoy our opening ceremony, and lots of fantastic discounts on our opening day.

77. What will people be able to enjoy on the opening day of the new supermarket?
(A) Extended opening hours
(B) Free food and drink
(C) A musical performance
(D) People dancing with ribbons

78. What can people NOT find at the Deli section?
(A) Meals to take out
(B) Fresh beef
(C) A place to sit and eat
(D) Food from overseas

Questions 79-80 refer to the following letter.

CompuFix Corp
Suite 34, Valerio Tower, 483 Bradshaw Blvd., Sacramento CA 94230
Tel 916-8754-5473

Mr. Cyril Edwards
GFS Furniture Supplies
3785 Robertson Street
Fresno, CA 93650

August 6, 2008

Dear Mr. Edwards,

I am writing to let you know about a problem with an order we made with your company for some office furniture (order #4699570). On July 10, we sent you an order for six office chairs, model OC5475, which are advertised on your website for $95.99 each. As promised, delivery was made within one week of the order. However, when we opened the boxes, we found that you had supplied us with only five chairs. Not only that, they were not the chairs we ordered. The chairs you sent us were model OC4755, which are similar to the OC5475 but cheaper and less comfortable. When we examined your invoice, however, we found you had charged us for our original order, i.e. six of the more expensive chairs.

Of course, we immediately called your customer service center to report the mistake. Your company sent a truck the following day to take away the wrong chairs and deliver the correct ones. However, this is the second time this year that your company has made a mistake with one of our orders. If this happens again, we will have to consider looking for a new supplier despite the long relationship between our two companies.

Marsha Halloran
CEO

---

79. What is the purpose of this letter?
    (A) To order some office chairs
    (B) To complain about poor service
    (C) To ask for a discount on merchandise
    (D) To let GFS know the merchandise hasn't arrived

80. What mistake was made with the client's order?
    (A) Delivery was late.
    (B) A more expensive model was delivered.
    (C) The wrong chairs were delivered twice.
    (D) Both the quantity and model were wrong.

➡ GO ON TO THE NEXT PAGE.

"RUN FOR LIFE"

SPONSORSHIP FORM

Winchester International Marathon

We thank you for choosing to run for charity! Please fill in this form and make sure you return a copy of it to the Winchester International Marathon office. We wish to keep track of your efforts and report them later in our 'RUN FOR LIFE' magazine. After the race you will receive a certificate from us. Good luck!

Name of applicant and runner: Daniella King
Phone Number: 020-8563-9980   E-mail: dking250@telbank.co.uk
Address: 57 Trafalgar Parade, London N16 5GT

Runner's Message
I'm participating in the race to raise money for my favorite charity, Doctors Without Borders. I hope that you'll help me raise funds by sponsoring my participation. This is my first ever marathon, so if I don't finish the race, just pay me for the part I completed! Thank you!

List of Sponsors for Daniella King

Sponsor's Name & Amount Offered		Amount Paid After the Race
1. Bruce Hurd	£50	£50
2. Val Graham	£40	£40
3. Kumar Trehan	£100	£100
4. Pat O'Malley	£50	£50
5. Klaus Schmidt	£80	
6. Maria Suarez	£30	£30
7. Keith Evans	£120	£150
8. Fiona Moore	£40	

81. How much of the race did Daniella King probably complete?
    (A) All of it
    (B) Some of it
    (C) Half of it
    (D) One quarter of it

82. Why is Daniella King taking part in this race?
    (A) Because she needs the money
    (B) Because she loves to run marathons
    (C) Because her friends asked her to
    (D) Because she wants to help people

83. What is true about Daniella King's sponsors?
    (A) Everyone has paid her except one person.
    (B) The three biggest sponsors have all paid her.
    (C) Everyone promised to pay more than £50.
    (D) One person paid more than he or she promised.

84. The phrase "keep track of" in line 2 is closest in meaning to
    (A) praise
    (B) follow
    (C) record on video
    (D) write about

➡ GO ON TO THE NEXT PAGE.

HOW TO QUIT SMOKING

1. Mark a day on your calendar for when you are going to quit smoking. Be sure to tell all of your family and friends about your attempt so they can support you.

2. Make some sensible preparations. Get rid of all your cigarettes and ashtrays. You'll probably miss the feeling of a cigarette in your mouth, so prepare some substitutes for cigarettes, such as sugarless gum, carrot sticks, or hard candies.

3. Attend a quit-smoking class. Practice saying, "No, thank you. I don't smoke." If you have tried to give up smoking in the past, think about what helped you before and what didn't help you.

4. Find people to support you in your effort to quit. These people could be friends or family members who have successfully stopped smoking. If you have friends and family who still smoke, ask them politely not to smoke around you.

5. Participate in the fun events organized by the National Anti-Smoking Society. Some past events include a campaign that encouraged smokers to hand over unfinished packs of cigarettes in exchange for a free gift.

6. Don't try to go too fast. Quit smoking for 24 hours. Use this as a starting point to help you quit for life. Make some new non-smoking friends, or find others who are trying to quit so you can help each other quit forever.

85. What advice is given to people who want to quit smoking?
(A) Do not go to places where people smoke.
(B) Try not to smoke for at least one week.
(C) Get help from friends and relatives.
(D) Become a member of the National Anti-Smoking Society.

86. In this passage, what is NOT mentioned as a way to give up smoking?
(A) Consult a doctor
(B) Throw away your cigarettes
(C) Join a group of people trying to quit
(D) Try to do it slowly

87. What is one thing people should do to help themselves quit smoking?
(A) Mark their calendar on days they didn't smoke.
(B) Give up gum and candy also.
(C) Practice refusing cigarettes.
(D) Read books about celebrities who have also quit.

Questions 88-90 refer to the following e-mail.

Date: January 4, 2009
To: Yvonne DeMarco, Vice President of Sales
From: Brent Oswald, Regional Sales Manager
Subject: Additional destination

Dear Yvonne,

I wanted to ask you if I could extend my upcoming trip to Europe. As you know, I'm going to Switzerland to discuss next year's production plan with our partners there. At the moment, I'm planning to leave on February 25 and return on March 2. However, I just heard that our partner in Germany is having financial problems. I'm not sure how serious these problems are, but I think it would be a good idea for me to go to Frankfurt to discuss the matter with the company face to face. I can't leave earlier because of the sales conference on February 23. I would therefore like to extend my stay in Europe and go to Germany after I visit Switzerland. I could leave Geneva on March 1 and fly to Frankfurt. I would probably have to spend two days there, and so I would get back to Chicago on March 4. Could you let me know if this will be OK? Meanwhile, I'll find out as much as I can about the problems of the German company, and I'll send you a report.

Thanks,
Brent

88. Why did Brent Oswald send this message?
(A) To inform his boss of his plan to make a business trip
(B) To inform his boss about a possible change of plans
(C) To give his boss a report about a German company
(D) To ask his boss to go with him to Europe

89. What does Brent Oswald want to do?
(A) Attend a sales conference, go to Switzerland, then go to Germany
(B) Go to Chicago, attend a sales conference, then fly to Frankfurt

(C) Go to Germany, then to Switzerland and return to Chicago
(D) Go to Switzerland, go to Germany, then attend a sales conference

90. What does Brent find out about their partner company in Germany?
(A) They feel satisfied with the German company.
(B) They think the German company is not doing well.
(C) They want to continue doing business with the German company.
(D) They want to stop doing business with the German company.

➡ GO ON TO THE NEXT PAGE.

EastMed Travel

EastMed Travel is an independent tour operator focusing on a variety of vacations including diving excursions and wedding packages, in Greece, Cyprus, Turkey and Egypt. We promise a warm welcome for all our customers in all of our destinations. EastMed guarantees that when customers arrive at their destinations, one of our representatives will always be readily available to answer questions about the resort or about local facilities and excursions.

Our main priority is to offer our customers quality service combined with a price they can afford. Having started our business in 1981, we have become well established in the markets in which we operate, and have a lot of experience in our specialist destinations. All of our employees fully understand the importance of our customers. We are careful to hire only representatives with a positive, helpful attitude and good communication skills.

So don't delay—visit our website at www.eastmedtravel.com or call Kevin at our New York Office 1-222-355-0331 to find out how you can book your holiday of a lifetime!

Date: August 6, 2008
To: kevin_grayson@eastmed.co.uk
From: cnoonan@bright.net
Subject: Your local representative

Dear Kevin,

I booked a holiday with your company, and I'm now staying with two friends at the Delphi Hotel in Larnaca, Cyprus. According to your advertisement, all of your local representatives are positive and helpful with good communication skills. I regret to inform you that this is certainly not true about your representative here. We were expecting him to meet us at the airport and take us to our hotel. He was nowhere to be found and we had to take a taxi. When we finally met him, he said that he was expecting us to arrive on the following day. We arranged a scuba diving excursion yesterday, but he arrived late and only brought enough equipment for two people, not three. He then spent the next hour finding one more set. In the end, our excursion was cut from a full day to half a day. My friends and I are extremely disappointed with the service your company is offering despite the promises you made in your publicity.

Claire Noonan

91. What kind of vacations does EastMed Travel specialize in?
(A) Trips to all parts of the world
(B) Outdoor vacations only
(C) Trips to one particular region
(D) Vacations for senior citizens

92. What special features does EastMed Travel mention in its publicity?
(A) Low prices and comfortable hotels
(B) Excellent service and good food
(C) Good food and a variety of activities
(D) Reasonable prices and high-quality service

93. What was Claire Noonan's first problem?
(A) She was taken to the wrong hotel.
(B) No one met her at the airport.
(C) Her flight arrived late.
(D) The hotel was not expecting her.

94. What was the problem with the scuba diving excursion?
(A) It was delayed by the mistakes of the representative.
(B) The representative brought the wrong kind of equipment.
(C) They couldn't get back to the hotel during the day.
(D) The representative did not meet them.

95. In the advertisement, the phrase "main priority" in line 6, is closest in meaning to
(A) favorite activity
(B) longest experience
(C) most profitable business
(D) most important aim

➡ *GO ON TO THE NEXT PAGE.*

G & L Industries

3317 Huntingdon Road, Springfield, IL 62704, U.S.A.

Phone 217-9873-0081; Fax 217-9873-0085

Mr. Mohinder Singh
PTC Co., Ltd.
Unit 38, Godiva Business Park
Siskin Road
Coventry CV1 5TY
UK

April 24, 2008

Dear Mr. Singh,

Thanks for your recent sales report. I'm glad to know that our products are selling well, and that our business relationship has gotten off to such a good start.

I am writing to let you know that I'm planning to visit the UK in June. I haven't been there for almost two years now. I want to spend some time in London looking around some of the major shopping centers so that I can experience the changing conditions in the retail market. After that, I'd like to go to Coventry and visit you at your company. I think it would be really helpful for me to see how your operation works and to meet some of your staff. I will be coming with Ms. Dana Metzger, who is head of our international sales section, and we would like to meet some people in your sales section to discuss some possible new strategies for the UK market.

I would be very grateful if you could let me know what your schedule is in mid-June so that I can arrange my visit at a convenient time for both of us.

I look forward to hearing from you.

Sincerely,

Leon Rausch
Leon Rausch
CEO

PTC Co., Ltd.
Unit 38, Godiva Business Park
Siskin Road, Coventry CV1 5TY
Phone: 24-7525-9523 Fax: 24-7524-6646

G & L Industries
3317 Huntingdon Road,
Springfield, IL 62704
USA

April 29, 2008

Dear Mr. Rausch,

Thank you very much for your letter. I'm also delighted that sales are going well. The first shipment we got from you is now almost completely sold out, and so we plan to make a new order around the middle of next month.

I was happy to hear that you'll be coming to visit us. There are a lot of things we need to talk about, and it is always better to do so face to face. We also have some new ideas for how to market your products more effectively in the UK market, and so we would be delighted to sit down and discuss this with you and Ms. Metzger. As regards a good time for your visit, I have to go to India to meet some clients from June 12 to 20. Would it be possible for you to arrange your visit on or after June 21?

I look forward to your reply.

Yours sincerely,

Mohinder Singh
Mohinder Singh
Managing Director

➡ *GO ON TO THE NEXT PAGE.*

96. What is the relationship between the two companies?
    (A) One is the parent company of the other.
    (B) One wants to take over the other.
    (C) They have a long-established business relationship.
    (D) They have just recently started doing business together.

97. When is the best time for Mr. Rausch to visit Mr. Singh's company?
    (A) June 21
    (B) Early June
    (C) Mid-June
    (D) Late June

98. What does Mr. Rausch want to do in London?
    (A) Visit Mr. Singh's company.
    (B) Look around some shops.
    (C) Have a sales meeting.
    (D) Sell his company's products.

99. What will Mr. Singh be doing in the middle of June?
    (A) Visiting overseas clients
    (B) Welcoming some clients from India
    (C) Preparing for a conference
    (D) Making a new order

100. In the first letter, the word "strategies" in paragraph 2, line 8, is closest in meaning to
    (A) figures
    (B) staff
    (C) plans
    (D) offices

Stop! This is the end of the test. If you finish before time is called, you may go back to Parts 5, 6, and 7 and check your work.

Half Test 1

100 題

LISTENING TEST（p. 30-38）

READING TEST （p. 39-54）把計時器設定為 38 分鐘。

LISTENING TEST 的 mp3 音軌從 Track 21 開始播放。

LISTENING TEST

In the Listening test, your will be asked to demonstrate how well you understand spoken English. The entire Listening test will last approximately 22 minutes. There are four parts, and directions are given for each part. You must mark your answers on the separate answer sheet. Do not write your answers in your test book.

Part 1

Directions: For each question in this part, you will hear four statements about a picture in your test book. When you hear the statements, you must select the one statement that best describes what you see in the picture. Then find the number of the question on your answer sheet and mark your answer. The statements will not be printed in your test book and will be spoken only one time.

Example

Sample Answer
Ⓐ Ⓑ ● Ⓓ

Statement (C), "They're standing near the table," is the best description of the picture, so you should select answer (C) and mark it on your answer sheet.

1.

2.

➡ *GO ON TO THE NEXT PAGE.*

3.

4.

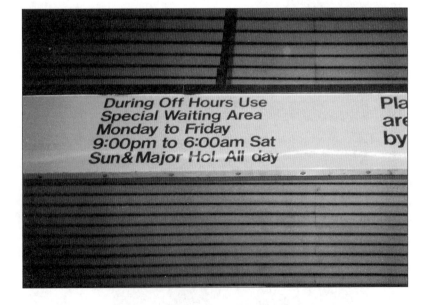

During Off Hours Use
Special Waiting Area
Monday to Friday
9:00pm to 6:00am Sat
Sun & Major Hol. All day

Pla
are
by

5.

➡ GO ON TO THE NEXT PAGE.

Pre Test

Half Test 1

Half Test 2

Full Test

Part 2

Directions: You will hear a question or statement and three responses spoken in English. They will not be printed in your test book and will be spoken only one time. Select the best response to the question or statement and mark the letter (A), (B), or (C) on your answer sheet.

Example

Sample Answer
Ⓐ ● Ⓒ

You will hear: Where is the meeting room?
You will also hear: (A) To meet the new director
                     (B) It's the first room on the right.
                     (C) Yes, at two o'clock.

The best response to the question "Where is the meeting room?" is choice (B), "It's the first room on the right," so (B) is the correct answer. You should mark answer (B) on your answer sheet.

6. Mark your answer on your answer sheet.

7. Mark your answer on your answer sheet.

8. Mark your answer on your answer sheet.

9. Mark your answer on your answer sheet.

10. Mark your answer on your answer sheet.

11. Mark your answer on your answer sheet.

12. Mark your answer on your answer sheet.

13. Mark your answer on your answer sheet.

14. Mark your answer on your answer sheet.

15. Mark your answer on your answer sheet.

16. Mark your answer on your answer sheet.

17. Mark your answer on your answer sheet.

18. Mark your answer on your answer sheet.

19. Mark your answer on your answer sheet.

20. Mark your answer on your answer sheet.

Part 3

Directions: You will hear some conversations between two people. You will be asked to answer three questions about what the speakers say in each conversation. Select the best response to each question and mark the letter (A), (B), (C), or (D) on your answer sheet. The conversations will not be printed in your test book and will be spoken only one time.

21. What kind of store is this?
    (A) An electronics store
    (B) A boutique
    (C) A furniture store
    (D) A jewelry store

22. What does the customer want to do?
    (A) To buy a gold chain
    (B) To exchange a sweater that has a hole in it
    (C) To return a silver pin
    (D) To look at chairs and sofas

23. What is the customer concerned about?
    (A) Price
    (B) Quality
    (C) Size
    (D) Brand

24. How many proposals do they have to present to Mr. Baines?
    (A) One
    (B) Three
    (C) Four
    (D) Five

25. Which of the proposals are they going to submit?
    (A) All of them
    (B) Everyone except proposal D
    (C) Everyone except proposals B and D
    (D) None of them

26. Why don't they like proposal D?
    (A) It's too expensive.
    (B) It's not original.
    (C) It's not innovative.
    (D) It's too abstractive.

➡ *GO ON TO THE NEXT PAGE.*

27. Where will the meeting that was originally scheduled for today take place?
    (A) At 9:00 tomorrow
    (B) At 10:00 tomorrow
    (C) In the conference room
    (D) In Mr. Jenkins' office

28. What does Mr. White ask his assistant to do?
    (A) Call the board meeting organizer.
    (B) Call the conference room.
    (C) Spend Friday at the conference.
    (D) Tell Mr. Jenkins he cannot see him.

29. What is Mr. White expected to do next?
    (A) Attend a conference
    (B) Go to the new plant
    (C) Meet Mr. Jenkins
    (D) Tell the board he is on his way

_____

30. Why does the man need help?
    (A) He wants to learn scuba diving.
    (B) He has to drive to the beach.
    (C) He wants to buy an apartment.
    (D) He is going to move.

31. Why can't the woman give an answer immediately?
    (A) She is not sure about her plans.
    (B) She does not want to cancel her appointment.
    (C) She does not want to help the man.
    (D) She is still wondering what to do.

32. What does the woman recommend that the man do?
    (A) Build up his strength.
    (B) Postpone the moving date.
    (C) Cancel the moving van the man reserved.
    (D) Talk to Takeshi about having him help.

33. Where does this conversation take place?
    (A) At a basketball game
    (B) On an airplane
    (C) At a ticket window
    (D) In a theater

34. Why could they not get better seats?
    (A) The tickets sold out quickly.
    (B) The performance took six hours.
    (C) They arrived too late.
    (D) The ticket agent was too busy.

35. What is the woman going to do?
    (A) Complain about the seats.
    (B) Enjoy the performance.
    (C) Guess why the seats are far from the stage.
    (D) Complain about the performance.

_____

Part 4

Directions: You will hear some talks given by a single speaker. You will be asked to answer three questions about what the speaker says in each talk. Select the best response to each question and mark the letter (A), (B), (C), or (D) on your answer sheet. The talks will not be printed in your test book and will be spoken only one time.

36. What problem is the speaker addressing?
    (A) One of the projects was canceled.
    (B) There is more work than they can handle.
    (C) Some members of the team are quitting.
    (D) The highway rest stop project has to be delayed.

37. What is the company's most important project?
    (A) The highway rest stop
    (B) The bridge design
    (C) Rearrangement of personnel
    (D) Rearrangement of the work schedule

38. How many members of the highway rest stop project will be transferred?
    (A) None
    (B) One
    (C) Three
    (D) Five

39. Where is this talk being given?
    (A) At a high school
    (B) At a medical clinic
    (C) At a police academy
    (D) At a driving school

40. How much time do they have to complete the essay?
    (A) Two hours and fifteen minutes
    (B) One hour and fifteen minutes
    (C) Forty minutes
    (D) Twenty minutes

41. Which of these areas is covered in part three of the test?
    (A) Automobile maintenance
    (B) Automobile designs
    (C) Buying a used car
    (D) Types of cars

GO ON TO THE NEXT PAGE.

42. Which of the following can you do at CoffeeNet Café?
   (A) Have as much coffee as you want.
   (B) Get a free cup of coffee if you bring your own laptop.
   (C) Log on to the Internet while your laptop is being repaired.
   (D) Buy a cup of coffee and check your e-mail.

43. How much is a cup of coffee at CoffeeNet Café?
   (A) $2.00
   (B) $2.25
   (C) $3.00
   (D) $3.25

44. Where is CoffeeNet Café located?
   (A) Between the university and the bank
   (B) Next to a bicycle shop
   (C) Across from a bank
   (D) On the university campus

45. Where did the plane go down?
   (A) At Dulles Airport in Washington
   (B) In Maryland
   (C) In the air
   (D) In the sea

46. Why are the rescue workers having difficulty?
   (A) The sea is rough and stormy.
   (B) The cause of the crash is not known.
   (C) The reports of a witness are unconfirmed.
   (D) The plane is on fire.

47. What is the rescue team looking for?
   (A) Witness of the accident
   (B) Airplane crew of the crashed plane
   (C) Survivers and the flight recorder
   (D) A telescope

48. What is taking place today?
   (A) A race
   (B) A track meet
   (C) A horse race
   (D) The 5,000-meter run

49. What event follows the 100-meter dash?
   (A) The 5,000-meter run
   (B) The 200-meter hurdles
   (C) The 10,000-meter run
   (D) The four-by 100-meter relay race

50. Who is this talk being addressed to?
   (A) The audience
   (B) The organizer of the track meet
   (C) Event staff members
   (D) The runners participating in the events

This is the end of the Listening test. Turn to Part 5 in your test book.

READING TEST

In the Reading test, you will read a variety of texts and answer several different types of reading comprehension questions. The entire Reading test will last 37 minutes. There are three parts, and directions are given for each part. You are encouraged to answer as many questions as possible within the time allowed.

You must mark your answers on the separate answer sheet. Do not write your answers in your test book.

Part 5

Directions: A word or phrase is missing in each of the sentences below. Four answer choices are given below each sentence. Select the best answer to complete the sentence. Then mark the letter (A), (B), (C), or (D) on your answer sheet.

51. ------- we know, Comtrex Corporation does not have a local distributor for its products in Malaysia.
    (A) As long as
    (B) As soon as
    (C) As far as
    (D) As much as

52. If the results of the laboratory tests are -------, the new drug is likely to win government approval.
    (A) satisfactory
    (B) satisfaction
    (C) satisfy
    (D) satisfied

53. Use of the gym facilities during the weekend will be 30 percent ------- the normal rates.
    (A) up
    (B) than
    (C) over
    (D) with

54. The goods we ordered on November 22 have not yet arrived, and we are concerned that they ------- in the mail.
    (A) may lose
    (B) may get lost
    (C) might get lost
    (D) may have gotten lost

55. After ------- low for two weeks, stock prices are beginning to show signs of recovery.
    (A) remain
    (B) remains
    (C) remaining
    (D) have remained

56. As head of the project team, Julia was responsible for ------- standards for the other members.
    (A) setting
    (B) placing
    (C) putting
    (D) achieving

➡ GO ON TO THE NEXT PAGE.

57. Having ------- the cram session for eight straight hours, the staff felt completely exhausted.
(A) attend
(B) attended
(C) attending
(D) attendant

58. Diabetes used to be a disease that affected mainly adults, but nowadays it ------- more and more common among children.
(A) is becoming
(B) becomes
(C) became
(D) will become

59. The congressman complained to the magazine, asking it to ------- a statement it published about his involvement with criminals.
(A) reject
(B) refuse
(C) recall
(D) retract

60. I'd like to speak to the person ------ customer relations for your company.
(A) charged with
(B) in charge of
(C) responsible to
(D) responsible in

61. Building costs in this area are at an all-time high, but rental prices have remained ------- steady.
(A) relating
(B) relation
(C) relative
(D) relatively

62. Our retailers are reluctant to lower their prices, but I think we should try to ------- them that this is actually a good idea.
(A) convince
(B) convict
(C) conform
(D) contact

63. No matter ------- hard he tried, Brian could not seem to achieve his monthly sales targets.
(A) very
(B) whether
(C) how
(D) more

64. The air conditioner needs ------- because it seems unable to maintain a constant temperature.
(A) to repair
(B) repairing
(C) repaired
(D) reparation

65. There is so little work between Christmas and New Year's that we ------- as well close the office for the entire period.
(A) can
(B) will
(C) may
(D) must

66. Consumer prices ------- for the first time in more than two years.
(A) have raised
(B) raised
(C) have risen
(D) have been rising

67. Only when sales figures get worse ------- to act.
(A) the head office began
(B) the head office would begin
(C) will the head office begin
(D) would the head office begin

68. A new state law prohibits people from using hand-held electronic communication devices ------- driving a car.
    (A) while
    (B) during
    (C) by
    (D) for

69. One great ------- for companies to set up in the new business zone is a lower tax rate.
    (A) increase
    (B) incentive
    (C) reward
    (D) feature

70. There are now high-speed plants that are ------- filling 300 bottles of juice per minute.
    (A) able to
    (B) possible to
    (C) capable of
    (D) suitable for

➡ GO ON TO THE NEXT PAGE.

Pre Test

Half Test 1

Half Test 2

Full Test

Part 6

Directions: Read the texts that follow. A word or phrase is missing in some of the sentences. Four answer choices are given below each of these sentences. Select the best answer to complete the text. Then mark the letter (A), (B), (C), or (D) on your answer sheet.

Questions 71-73 refer to the following article.

Eating well in the UK

Britain is no longer the poor relation of the world as far as good food is -------. Bland flavors,

71. (A) related
    (B) concerned
    (C) connected
    (D) respected

overcooked vegetables and weak coffee are now a thing of the past. London in particular is currently home to many of the world's finest restaurants, serving some of the most innovative and inventive dishes to be found anywhere.

Dining in London's top-class restaurants, however, is far from cheap. If you want to eat well on a lower budget, it is worth investigating the food of Britain's immigrant communities. Indian cuisine, for example, has become so popular over the last 20 years or so, that it has virtually established itself as the country's favorite food. Most towns and cities have restaurants offering excellent Indian and Chinese food, as well as Middle Eastern and Caribbean food in larger cities, all at very ------- prices.

72. (A) average
    (B) rational
    (C) common
    (D) reasonable

In the medium-to-expensive price range, there is a good selection of Italian and French restaurants. Spanish tapas bars are now springing up in more fashionable urban areas, and more and more Japanese restaurants can now be found, ------- these are still quite expensive.

73. (A) even
    (B) despite
    (C) though
    (D) however

Questions 74-76 refer to the following e-mail.

Date: September 30, 2008
To: fhall@hallbrothers.com
From: janice@treetop.com
Subject: Roof repair

Dear Mr. Hall,

I'm sorry to inform you that my roof is leaking again. It was fine after you repaired it in July, but as you know, we had a very heavy rainstorm on Saturday. -------, water has started coming in again.

74. (A) On the other hand
(B) By the way
(C) In spite of that
(D) As a result

However, I'm sure my landlord will cover all the repair costs. He owns the house, and so the responsibility for the repairs is his. But he said that before he can make a decision, he must have an estimate for the cost of the work. I would therefore be very grateful if you could take a look ------- possible and let me know how much the repairs will cost.

75. (A) as long as
(B) as well as
(C) as soon as
(D) as much as

The problem is not as bad as before, but the longer we leave it, the ------- it will get. Please let me know when you can take a look.

76. (A) worse
(B) bad
(C) better
(D) worth

Kind regards,
Janice Stapleton

➡ GO ON TO THE NEXT PAGE.

Part 7

Directions: In this part, you will read a selection of texts, such as magazine and newspaper articles, letters and advertisements. Each text is followed by several questions. Select the best answer for each question and mark the letter (A), (B), (C), or (D) on your answer sheet.

Questions 77-78 refer to the following notice.

BRASSERIE DE PARIS CLOSED FOR REMODELING

All of us at Brasserie de Paris would like to thank all our customers for your continued support over the past five years since we opened. In fact, your support has been so good that we no longer have enough room for everyone! To ensure that you will no longer have to put up with long waiting times and small tables, we have finally decided to expand the restaurant. We are very sorry, but we will be closed for two weeks, from Monday, August 4 to Sunday, August 17, while we remodel the restaurant. Not only will we be building a new outdoor dining terrace with enough room for 30 customers, but we'll also be installing a complete new state-of-the-art kitchen. And at the same time as remodeling the restaurant, we'll also be remodeling the menu. All your old favorites will still be available, but our new award-winning chef, Marcel Roussel, will be adding some delicious new creations. We're sorry for the inconvenience, but we're sure that our restaurant is going to be even better as a result.

77. What is happening to the restaurant?
   (A) It is moving to another location to improve its business.
   (B) It is reducing the number of employees.
   (C) It is expanding the restaurant space to accommodate more customers.
   (D) It is replacing its current menu with a completely new one.

78. The word "state-of-the-art" in line 8 is closest in meaning to
   (A) down-to-earth
   (B) up-to-date
   (C) spacious
   (D) decorative

Questions 79-82 refer to the following notice.

Workplace Safety

All operations must be planned to prevent accidents. Please observe the following rules.

(a) All employees must report unsafe conditions or practices to their supervisors. If your supervisor does not take a corrective action immediately, employees must contact the Risk Management Department.

(b) The work area must be kept as clean and tidy as possible at all times.

(c) Suitable clothing, headgear and footwear must be worn at all times.

(d) All employees are expected to attend one safety meeting conducted by their supervisors.

(e) Anyone under the influence of alcohol or drugs, including prescription drugs, will not be allowed to enter the work area.

(f) Employees should make sure that all protective devices are properly positioned and adjusted.

(g) When lifting heavy objects, use the large muscles of the leg, not the smaller muscles of the back.

(h) Do not throw things on the ground. Dispose of all waste properly and carefully.

➡ GO ON TO THE NEXT PAGE.

Pre Test

Half Test 1

Half Test 2

Full Test

79. What must employees do first if they find themselves in dangerous conditions?
    (A) Contact the Risk Management Department.
    (B) Inform their supervisor.
    (C) Take corrective action.
    (D) Attend a safety meeting.

80. In what instance should workers get in touch with the Risk Management Department?
    (A) When directed by their supervisor to do so
    (B) When the supervisor does not take rapid corrective action
    (C) When unsafe conditions are discovered
    (D) When there is a safety meeting

81. How often do workers have to participate in safety meetings?
    (A) At least once
    (B) Whenever they think it is necessary
    (C) Whenever a meeting is held
    (D) If the Risk Management Department tells them to

82. What kind of workers are NOT prohibited from entering the workplace?
    (A) Those who have drunk alcohol
    (B) Those not wearing the correct clothing
    (C) Those who cannot drive
    (D) Those who have taken strong medication

Questions 83-86 refer to the following advertisement.

Golden Wedding Package

(*Based on minimum 100 guests*)

Our Golden Wedding Package provides a superb wedding experience with 'everything but the groom' included. This package will set you free from any stress associated with planning a wedding reception. With more than 30 years of experience, our expert staff will assist and guide you in planning an unforgettable event to help you celebrate that most special day!

This package includes:

Five Hours of Continuous Music with Band

Wine, Champagne & Chocolate Favors

Wine poured during dinner with champagne toast and ribbon-tied chocolate favors for all guests

Limousine Service

8-passenger limousine—black or white

Complete service from home to ceremony, champagne, red carpet, chauffeur and 3 hours of service

Tuxedos

$80.00 per person

Free tuxedo for the groom and $20.00 off each additional tuxedo for members of wedding party (minimum order of 5)

Invitations

A wonderful selection including invitations to the reception, response and thank-you cards

Call for pricing.

➡ GO ON TO THE NEXT PAGE.

83. Who is the Golden Wedding Package designed for?
   (A) A couple 30 years old or above
   (B) A couple celebrating their wedding anniversary
   (C) A couple with 100 guests or more
   (D) A couple who do not want to spend a lot

84. What does the company stress about itself?
   (A) It is cheaper than its competitors.
   (B) It can arrange weddings for groups of any size.
   (C) It specializes in providing gourmet food.
   (D) It has a lot of experience.

85. What is the cost of tuxedos for the groom and three guests?
   (A) $180
   (B) $240
   (C) It depends on the season.
   (D) The service is not available.

86. What can guests enjoy throughout the party?
   (A) Live music
   (B) Limousine service
   (C) Beautiful thank-you cards
   (D) Many different meal choices

Questions 87-90 refer to the following instructions.

The following fire emergency procedures should be followed by all employees in the event of a fire or explosion:

If you discover a fire or see smoke:

1 Remove all visitors and employees from the immediate danger area.

2 Activate the fire alarm system.

3 Dial 9999 (Control Center) and report:

(a) the EXACT location of the fire (building, floor and room number);
(b) the type of fire (electrical, flammable liquid, trash, etc.);
(c) the extent of the fire (severity of fire and/or amount of smoke);
(d) your name.

4 If you feel capable, attempt to extinguish the fire using the proper fire extinguisher.

5 Confine the fire and smoke by closing all windows and doors.

6 DO NOT LOCK THE DOOR. LEAVE THE CORRIDOR AND ROOM LIGHTS ON.

7 If possible, shut off all nonessential gas and electrical appliances in the area and remove any hazardous materials.

8 Evacuate the building using the nearest enclosed stairway or ground exit if fire and smoke cannot be controlled, or if YOU think it is necessary.

9 Reenter the building only after the all-clear is signaled by repeated intermittent sounds on the building alarm system.

Building personnel should work as a team to accomplish the above procedures.

➡ *GO ON TO THE NEXT PAGE.*

87. In case of fire, what must employees do
    first?
    (A) Call the nearest fire station.
    (B) Evacuate guests and co-workers.
    (C) Try to bring the fire under control.
    (D) Sound an alarm.

88. Why do employees have to close all
    windows and doors?
    (A) To stop the fire from spreading
    (B) To make it easy to extinguish the fire
    (C) To determine the exact location of the
        fire
    (D) To judge how severe the fire is

89. What must employees do if they think the
    fire cannot be controlled?
    (A) Activate the fire alarm.
    (B) Make sure all doors are unlocked.
    (C) Turn off unnecessary appliances.
    (D) Just leave the building from the
        closest exit.

90. When can employees reenter the
    building?
    (A) When the alarm rings continuously
    (B) When the alarm rings on and off
    (C) When the fire department says it is
        safe to do so
    (D) When they can no longer see smoke

Questions 91-95 refer to the following announcement and memo.

GRANT PLAZA CONFERENCE CENTER

The Grant Plaza Conference Center is proud of its convenient location in the heart of the city's business district. It charges a per-person conference rate of $80.00 plus occupancy tax. The basic plan includes the following:

I.   Meeting space with state-of-the-art, built-in audiovisual and conference equipment
II. Rooms equipped with executive chairs and conference tables set up in your preferred pattern
III. Light breakfast, lunch buffet, and mid-afternoon refreshment break
IV. Conference supplies including pencils, note pads, flip charts, pushpins and markers
V.   A Conference Planner to coordinate all your needs from room set-up to dinner service
VI. Additional services such as photocopying, faxing and secretarial assistance are available at the Business Center

* If you require video-conferencing, teleconferencing or simultaneous interpretation, your Conference Planner will inform you of the additional cost.

OFFICE MEMO

To: Bruce Forman
From: Larry Thielemans
Subject: Research on conference center

Take a look at the information on the Grant Plaza Conference Center I've attached to this memo. I think it might be worth considering it as a possible location for this year's research conference.

I know we've been using the Pacific Heights Center for some years now, but quite frankly, I think we need a change. Standards at the Pacific Heights Center are dropping. I was there for another conference a few weeks ago, and I wasn't impressed. It's starting to look old and run-down. What's more, the projection system broke down in the middle of a presentation. It took about half an hour to fix it, and so everything ended up running late. The food was nothing special, either.

On the other hand, the Grant Plaza Conference Center hasn't been operating for very long, but its reputation is growing. I know it's more expensive than Pacific Heights, but we may be able to negotiate a better rate if we can convince them that we want a long-term relationship. Also, we'll have some very important influential guests at this year's conference, and we need to do our best to impress them.

Let me know what you think.
Larry

➡ *GO ON TO THE NEXT PAGE.*

91. What is NOT included in the basic price of the conference center?
    (A) Meal service
    (B) Simultaneous interpretation
    (C) Audiovisual equipment
    (D) Stationery

92. Why is Larry Thieleman suggesting a change of the place?
    (A) The Grant Plaza Conference Center has offered a discount.
    (B) The Pacific Heights Conference Center has increased its rates.
    (C) He is unhappy with the present conference center.
    (D) The Grant Plaza Conference Center is in a more convenient location.

93. What must conference participants do if they want photocopies?
    (A) Go to the Business Center.
    (B) Ask the Conference Planner.
    (C) Use the copy machine in the conference room.
    (D) Pay an additional fee.

94. What problem did Larry Thielemans recently experience at a conference?
    (A) The computer system crashed.
    (B) There was not enough food.
    (C) The standards dropped.
    (D) A projector stopped working.

95. How would Larry Thielemans approach the new convention center for a cheaper rate?
    (A) By mentioning its inconvenient access
    (B) By mentioning his company's wish to keep using it for a long time
    (C) By mentioning the possibility of holding a big conference there
    (D) By mentioning the poor quality of the equipment

Questions 96-100 refer to the following two e-mail messages.

From: fdavies@earth.com
To: rdarcy@link.com
Subject: New business venture?

Hi, Ruth. How have you been? I know we haven't been in touch for a while, but I thought I'd sound you out on an idea for a new business that I've been thinking about.

Have you been to the new business park that opened up in Carlton last year? I had to go out there last week. I had some free time, and so I thought I'd drive around and take a look at it. There are lots of companies out there now and also a few restaurants, but I didn't notice a single sandwich shop. I think a good sandwich shop there would do tremendous business. What we would need to do is find a kitchen where we could prepare the sandwiches in the morning, and then put some kind of ordering and delivery system and a small stall in place.

I used to love working in the catering business, and now that the kids are older, I'd love a chance to get back into it. I think this is a fantastic opportunity, but I can't do it alone. I really need a reliable partner with a good background in food, and you're the obvious choice. Let me know if you're interested.

Best wishes,

Fiona Davies

From: rdarcy@link.com
To: fdavies@earth.com
Subject: Re: New business venture?

Dear Fiona,

It was great to hear from you. You have a wonderful sense of timing, I must say! I've been a bit restless since Jerry and I sold the restaurant, and I'd love to get back into business again. I think your plan sounds good, and I've already done a bit of research.

Do you remember my friend Tommy Davidson? He's just opened a new restaurant not far from the business park in Carlton, and he's agreed to let us use his kitchen in the morning. I also re-established contact with some of our old suppliers, and so I know I can get high-quality ingredients at very reasonable prices. There are still a lot of things to think about, such as the ordering and delivery system, menu and pricing. It will be hard work, but I'm sure we could set up a very successful little business without having to spend too much money.

Let's get together soon and discuss it.

Ruth D'Arcy

➡ GO ON TO THE NEXT PAGE.

96. What do the two women want to do?
    (A) Open a restaurant.
    (B) Open a sandwich business.
    (C) Move to Carlton.
    (D) Sell their restaurant.

97. Which statement best describes
    experience in their food business?
    (A) They both have experience.
    (B) Neither of them has experience.
    (C) Fiona has experience, but Ruth does
        not.
    (D) Ruth has experience, but Fiona does
        not.

98. Why does Fiona want Ruth for her
    business partner?
    (A) Ruth is trustworthy and experienced.
    (B) Ruth has no job at the moment.
    (C) Ruth and her husband are her old
        friends.
    (D) Ruth is hard-working and energetic.

99. Who is Tommy Davidson?
    (A) A sandwich shop owner
    (B) The women's business partner
    (C) A restaurant owner
    (D) Ruth's husband

100. What is Ruth's reaction to Fiona's plan for
     a new business?
    (A) She thinks it will be easy.
    (B) She does not think it will be
        successful.
    (C) She thinks it will be expensive but
        successful.
    (D) She thinks it will be difficult but
        successful.

**Stop! This is the end of the test. If you finish before time is called, you may go
back to Parts 5, 6, and 7 and check your work.**

Half Test 2

100 題

LISTENING TEST（p. 56-64）
READING TEST　（p. 65-79）把計時器設定為 38 分鐘。

LISTENING TEST 的 ◎ mp3 音軌從 Track 37 開始播放。

LISTENING TEST

In the Listening test, your will be asked to demonstrate how well you understand spoken English. The entire Listening test will last approximately 22 minutes. There are four parts, and directions are given for each part. You must mark your answers on the separate answer sheet. Do not write your answers in your test book.

Part 1

Directions: For each question in this part, you will hear four statements about a picture in your test book. When you hear the statements, you must select the one statement that best describes what you see in the picture. Then find the number of the question on your answer sheet and mark your answer. The statements will not be printed in your test book and will be spoken only one time.

Example   Sample Answer

                                                                             Ⓐ Ⓑ ● Ⓓ

Statement (C), "They're standing near the table," is the best description of the picture, so you should select answer (C) and mark it on your answer sheet.

1.

2.

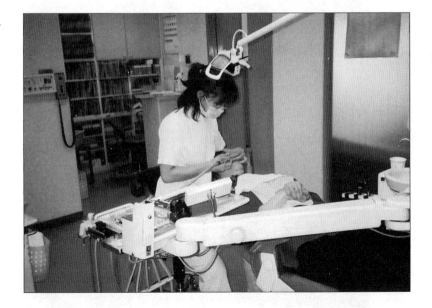

➡ GO ON TO THE NEXT PAGE.

3.

4.

5.

➡ GO ON TO THE NEXT PAGE.

Pre Test

Half Test 1

Half Test 2

Full Test

Part 2

Directions: You will hear a question or statement and three responses spoken in English. They will not be printed in your test book and will be spoken only one time. Select the best response to the question or statement and mark the letter (A), (B), or (C) on your answer sheet.

Example

Sample Answer
Ⓐ ● Ⓒ

You will hear:　　　Where is the meeting room?
You will also hear: (A) To meet the new director
　　　　　　　　　(B) It's the first room on the right.
　　　　　　　　　(C) Yes, at two o'clock.

The best response to the question "Where is the meeting room?" is choice (B), "It's the first room on the right," so (B) is the correct answer. You should mark answer (B) on your answer sheet.

6. Mark your answer on your answer sheet.

7. Mark your answer on your answer sheet.

8. Mark your answer on your answer sheet.

9. Mark your answer on your answer sheet.

10. Mark your answer on your answer sheet.

11. Mark your answer on your answer sheet.

12. Mark your answer on your answer sheet.

13. Mark your answer on your answer sheet.

14. Mark your answer on your answer sheet.

15. Mark your answer on your answer sheet.

16. Mark your answer on your answer sheet.

17. Mark your answer on your answer sheet.

18. Mark your answer on your answer sheet.

19. Mark your answer on your answer sheet.

20. Mark your answer on your answer sheet.

Part 3

Directions: You will hear some conversations between two people. You will be asked to answer three questions about what the speakers say in each conversation. Select the best response to each question and mark the letter (A), (B), (C), or (D) on your answer sheet. The conversations will not be printed in your test book and will be spoken only one time.

21. Who does the man call?
    (A) An Internet subscriber
    (B) An electronic appliance store
    (C) An Internet service provider
    (D) A CD rental shop

22. What does the woman ask the man?
    (A) If she can help him
    (B) What steps he has taken
    (C) To tell her what he is doing
    (D) To tell her what is wrong

23. What has the man NOT done before calling the woman?
    (A) Followed installation instructions
    (B) Restarted the computer
    (C) Put the CD-ROM in
    (D) Sent an e-mail requesting help

24. What is the man's problem?
    (A) The cashier did not give him a receipt.
    (B) He was charged for something he did not buy.
    (C) He is angry with the cashier.
    (D) An item was missing from his cart.

25. What does the cashier recommend?
    (A) Going over to the entrance
    (B) Asking about his receipt
    (C) Checking with the service counter
    (D) Leaving her alone

26. According to the man, who is responsible for the problem?
    (A) The cashier
    (B) The owner of the store
    (C) The service counter
    (D) The salesperson

➡ GO ON TO THE NEXT PAGE.

27. Where does this conversation take place?
    (A) At a home improvement center
    (B) At a hotel lobby
    (C) At an airport
    (D) At a restaurant

28. How long will the customers have to wait?
    (A) For half an hour
    (B) About 6 minutes
    (C) Until 11:00
    (D) Until 12:00

29. What are they going to do after this conversation?
    (A) Board the plane
    (B) Have drinks at the bar
    (C) Get in line
    (D) Reserve a window seat

30. What's the soonest the supplier can ship the entire order?
    (A) The 16th
    (B) The 18th
    (C) The 21st
    (D) The 23rd

31. What is Mr. Thomas going to tell the supplier?
    (A) Have the entire order shipped by the 23rd
    (B) Ship on time or they will lose the order.
    (C) Ship what they have in stock.
    (D) That he wants to cancel the order.

32. Why do they need the entire shipment by the 18th?
    (A) For the trade show on the 21st
    (B) So Mr. Thomas won't get angry
    (C) Because the trade show will be over by then
    (D) Because they are going to contact another supplier

33. What is Ms. Smith worried about?
    (A) When she can see the doctor
    (B) Being late for her doctor's appointment
    (C) Having an operation
    (D) The date of a new appointment

34. How long will Ms. Smith have to wait?
    (A) Until 9:30
    (B) Until the doctor arrives
    (C) Twenty or thirty minutes
    (D) An hour

35. Who is Ms. Smith speaking to?
    (A) A doctor
    (B) A patient
    (C) A nurse
    (D) A pharmacist

Part 4

Directions: You will hear some talks given by a single speaker. You will be asked to answer three questions about what the speaker says in each talk. Select the best response to each question and mark the letter (A), (B), (C), or (D) on your answer sheet. The talks will not be printed in your test book and will be spoken only one time.

36. How does spam affect e-mail use?
    (A) It makes communication more efficient.
    (B) It makes communication easier.
    (C) Lots of junk mail annoys the users.
    (D) Lots of junk mail destroys the computer system.

37. What benefits does SpamBlaster offer?
    (A) It is free of charge.
    (B) It gets rid of spam 100%.
    (C) It is free for two weeks and easy to install.
    (D) The price is reduced to 75%.

38. What can the user do if not satisfied with the product after the trial period?
    (A) Simply stop using it.
    (B) Send it back to the company.
    (C) Write to the company.
    (D) Get the money back.

39. What kind of store is Something Buoyant?
    (A) A gift shop
    (B) A men's clothing store
    (C) A sporting goods store
    (D) A discount outlet

40. What kind of benefit comes with the purchase of an overcoat?
    (A) A free gift
    (B) A 20% discount
    (C) An invitation to a show
    (D) A gift certificate

41. What kind of shoppers does the advertisement target?
    (A) Easter shoppers
    (B) Christmas shoppers
    (C) Annual sale shoppers
    (D) Back-to-school shoppers

GO ON TO THE NEXT PAGE.

42. What disrupted the governor's speech?
    (A) A large turnout
    (B) An explosion
    (C) Police department officials
    (D) People running for safety

43. Who was responsible for the explosion?
    (A) The gas company.
    (B) High-school kids.
    (C) A group opposing his reelection.
    (D) No one knows for certain.

44. What did the governor say after the explosion?
    (A) He is planning to retire.
    (B) He will not stop campaigning.
    (C) He was shaken and terrified.
    (D) He didn't comment a word.

45. Who is this advertisement targeted specifically towards?
    (A) Internet providers
    (B) Computer engineers
    (C) People who are not happy with their Internet providers
    (D) People with technical experience

46. How many customers does the provider serve?
    (A) Nearly one million
    (B) Over one million
    (C) One hundred million
    (D) One hundred

47. What does the FiberViper offer?
    (A) Fast connection service
    (B) A big discount on the monthly fee
    (C) Free update information
    (D) Free trial period

48. Where is this speech being made?
    (A) At a sport event
    (B) At a company party
    (C) At someone's office
    (D) At an award presentation ceremony

49. How did the company do this year?
    (A) It was very successful.
    (B) It tried very hard.
    (C) It was presented with an award.
    (D) Its income doubled.

50. What kind of person is the speaker most likely?
    (A) A celebrity
    (B) A senior employee
    (C) An award winner
    (D) A high-level executive

This is the end of the Listening test. Turn to Part 5 in your test book.

READING TEST

In the Reading test, you will read a variety of texts and answer several different types of reading comprehension questions. The entire Reading test will last 37 minutes. There are three parts, and directions are given for each part. You are encouraged to answer as many questions as possible within the time allowed.

You must mark your answers on the separate answer sheet. Do not write your answers in your test book.

Part 5

Directions: A word or phrase is missing in each of the sentences below. Four answer choices are given below each sentence. Select the best answer to complete the sentence. Then mark the letter (A), (B), (C), or (D) on your answer sheet.

51. Applicants for this assignment must be aged between 22 and 30, and -------.
    (A) physical fit
    (B) physically fit
    (C) physical fitting
    (D) physically fitting

52. The problem ------- easier to solve if damage caused by pollution were restricted to only this area.
    (A) will be
    (B) would be
    (C) was
    (D) is

53. Using e-mail instead of writing letters by hand is becoming more common, but it is ------- that all future communications will be electronic.
    (A) unusual
    (B) unuseful
    (C) unpopulalr
    (D) unlikely

54. It was so ------- of Meg to telll Ian that she would never go out with him no matter what.
    (A) inconsistent
    (B) inappropriate
    (C) insufficient
    (D) inconsiderate

55. Business customs in the United States differ significantly from ------- in Japan.
    (A) any
    (B) some
    (C) these
    (D) those

56. The company is likely to face ------- if it fails to win the new government contract.
    (A) bankrupt
    (B) bankruptcy
    (C) bankrupted
    (D) bankrupting

57. Advertising products is most ------ when it is approached as multi-media activity.
    (A) effect
    (B) effective
    (C) effectively
    (D) effectiveness

58. Oil inventories are well above normal, yet prices are almost twice as ------- as they were in the 1980s.
    (A) expensive
    (B) many
    (C) large
    (D) high

➡ *GO ON TO THE NEXT PAGE.*

59. The company decided to ------- its workers by giving an across-the-board pay raise.
    (A) reward
    (B) approve
    (C) refund
    (D) lay off

60. Jake Cornford always attributed his success in life to ------- out of college to pursue his dream.
    (A) falling
    (B) dropping
    (C) running
    (D) flying

61. The standard ------- period on this product is one year, but this can be extended up to five years with an additional payment.
    (A) security
    (B) discount
    (C) warranty
    (D) trial

62. One attractive feature of the apartment block is that it has a handyman ------- call 24 hours a day.
    (A) for
    (B) on
    (C) in
    (D) by

63. Our new series of basic tools is essential ------- small jobs around the house.
    (A) to do
    (B) to have done
    (C) for being done
    (D) for doing

64. We are proud of our reputation as being the benchmark ------- which all other facilities are measured.
    (A) at
    (B) for
    (C) upon
    (D) against

65. ------- the upward trend continues depends largely on the nation's economy and unemployment rate.
    (A) That
    (B) Which
    (C) Whether
    (D) What

66. The recent survey we conducted shows that people who invest in our company stock ------- salaries of between $50,000 and $100,000 annually.
    (A) gain
    (B) earn
    (C) win
    (D) take

67. The newly constructed port is located ------- a 90-minute drive of the region's two major airports.
    (A) inside
    (B) within
    (C) containing
    (D) entering

68. We had better leave the door ------- in case Jane and Tom do not have a key.
    (A) unlock
    (B) unlocking
    (C) unlocked
    (D) be unlocked

69. The Euro has recently declined in value ------- the yen.
    (A) against
    (B) with
    (C) for
    (D) toward

70. A drop in temperature of ------- 3 degrees Celsius would have a dramatic effect on life on Earth.
    (A) as many as
    (B) as high as
    (C) as much as
    (D) as little as

Part 6

Directions: Read the texts that follow. A word or phrase is missing in some of the sentences. Four answer choices are given below each of these sentences. Select the best answer to complete the text. Then mark the letter (A), (B), (C), or (D) on your answer sheet.

Questions 71-73 refer to the following letter.

Earthquake Appeal from Hands Across the Frontiers

Massive relief efforts are still ------- for the countless survivors of the recent earthquake.

71. (A) undergoing
    (B) underway
    (C) underweight
    (D) underground

We estimate that providing shelter, food, emergency financial assistance and medical services will cost more than $1 billion. Government assistance alone is not enough. It is up ------- organizations such as Hands Across the Frontiers and individuals.

72. (A) at
    (B) to
    (C) from
    (D) with

There are thousands of people in desperate ------- of assistance, and recovery will be a long and difficult task.

73. (A) need
    (B) necessity
    (C) necessary
    (D) necessitate

Your donations are vital in helping us continue to provide this much-needed help.

So far, we have provided more than $500 million in direct financial assistance to families in the form of food and shelter. But more help is needed for the relief efforts in the weeks and months ahead. Please give all you can to help.

➡ GO ON TO THE NEXT PAGE.

Pre Test

Half Test 1

Half Test 2

Full Test

Questions 74-76 refer to the following article.

"Fair Trading, A New Trend in Business"

Nowadays, many companies in developed countries are becoming interested in pursuing trading policy. --------, they try to make sure that their business operations do as little damage to

74. (A) However
    (B) On the other hand
    (C) On the contrary
    (D) In other words

people and the environment as possible, and at the same time, raise interest in what is necessary to improve standards of living worldwide.

Fair trade policies include the following rules:

Rule 1 Do not invest in countries where governments ------- people's human rights.

75. (A) stop
    (B) deny
    (C) quit
    (D) prohibit

Rule 2 Do not invest in companies whose activities harm the environment.
Rule 3 Do not invest in companies that ------- products on animals.

76. (A) test
    (B) examine
    (C) exercise
    (D) experience

Part 7

Directions: In this part, you will read a selection of texts, such as magazine and newspaper articles, letters and advertisements. Each text is followed by several questions. Select the best answer for each question and mark the letter (A), (B), (C), or (D) on your answer sheet.

Questions 77-80 refer to the following introduction.

Patrick J. Finley
Founder and Chief Executive Officer

Patrick Finley's multifaceted background in the entertainment industry includes more than 15 years of experience in licensing, production, contract law and finance. He founded Angel Entertainment in 2001, and under his leadership the company has become an influential youth-oriented entertainment brand. Besides being an accomplished producer, Mr. Finley is fluent in Japanese since he lived in Yokohama until he was 16. He frequently appears as a guest speaker at international conferences. Additionally, he has been a guest lecturer at universities in the United States and Japan.

As CEO and president of Angel Entertainment, Mr. Finley has raised over $15 million in equity, and has personally negotiated and completed licensing deals with dozens of international publishing, video game, animation and film companies.

Prior to founding Angel Entertainment, Mr. Finley was active in the creation and production of a number of innovative digital entertainment projects. Mr. Finley holds a B.A. in Economics from Seattle University. He began his career as an attorney after graduating from Midlands University Law Center and is a member of the Washington State Bar.

➡ *GO ON TO THE NEXT PAGE.*

77. What is Patrick J. Finley's main area of professional activity?
    (A) He is a lawyer.
    (B) He is an entertainer.
    (C) He is a company boss.
    (D) He is a university lecturer.

78. Which market does Angel Entertainment focus on?
    (A) Young people
    (B) The United States
    (C) Japan
    (D) International events

79. As CEO, what has Mr. Finley done for his company?
    (A) Issued stocks worth over $15 million
    (B) Signed contracts worth over $15 million
    (C) Set up branch offices in Japan
    (D) Collaborated with universities

80. When did Mr. Finley become involved in digital entertainment?
    (A) While he was a university student
    (B) Since going to Japan
    (C) Before setting up Angel Entertainment
    (D) After negotiating licensing deals

Questions 81-84 refer to the following advertisement.

Buy a TMR 3G mobile phone—get up to $50 back

Now, for a limited time, when you buy a TMR 3G mobile phone directly from TMR.com, you can get a $50 mail-in rebate if you sign up for a two-year service contract. Or get a $20 rebate with a one-year service contract. That means now you can get the hottest new 3G mobile phone around for as little as $99.

To take advantage of this offer, just:

1. Buy a TMR 3G mobile phone with new service activation from TMR.com between October 1, 2005 and December 31, 2005.

    IMPORTANT: Purchase price must be $149 or above to qualify for this rebate.

2. During plan selection, choose a two-year service contract for the $50 mail-in rebate or a one-year service contract for the $20 mail-in rebate.

3. When your TMR 3G mobile phone arrives, send the following items to the address on the form:
    Completed rebate form
    Copy of sales receipt or order confirmation e-mail
    Original barcode cut out from your TMR 3G mobile phone box
    (copies will not be accepted)

4. Enjoy your new TMR 3G mobile phone! Your mail-in rebate should arrive within 8 to 10 weeks. Checks must be cashed within 90 days of the issue date.

Pre Test

Half Test 1

Half Test 2

Full Test

➡ *GO ON TO THE NEXT PAGE.*

81. What is this passage telling people about?
    (A) A low-priced brand item
    (B) A clearance sale
    (C) A trade-in discount
    (D) A money-back offer for a limited time

82. What should people do to get a $50 cash-back bonus?
    (A) Buy a TMR 3G and apply for a two-year service period
    (B) Use a credit card to buy a TMR 3G
    (C) Cash a check within 90 days
    (D) Spend up to $149 on a TMR 3G

83. What items do people have to send to take advantage of this offer?
    (A) A completed rebate form, an original sales slip and barcode cut out from the box
    (B) A completed rebate form, copies of the sales slip and the barcode
    (C) A completed rebate form, a copy of the sales slip and an original barcode
    (D) A completed rebate form, copies of the sales slip and the order confirmation e-mail

84. Under what conditions does the rebate offer apply?
    (A) On 2-year service contracts only
    (B) On 1-year and 2-year service contracts
    (C) On any phone costing more than $99
    (D) On any phone purchased in 2005

Questions 85-87 refer to the following notice.

CITY OF REDBANK

Waste and Recycling

In order to cover a 32 percent increase in landfill charges, the city has had to increase its waste collection charges. However, the Waste Disposal Pass below entitles residents of the City of Redbank to dispose of specified domestic waste at the city dump free of charge.

The pass is for the use of City of Redbank residents only.

Waste Dump Operating Hours: 7:30 a.m. - 4:00 p.m., seven days a week, except for public holidays

Commercial businesses cannot dispose of commercial waste using domestic dump passes.

Residents who misplace or lose their Waste passes (as shown below) will be required to pay $30 in cash. This cash payment is non-refundable.

WASTE DISPOSAL PASS
City of Redbank
Property: ___325West Grayson Street, Redbank___

This pass may be used by city householders to dispose of one trailer of either Garden waste, or Plastic waste at the Redbank City Dump
(This pass is not transferable)

*The bearer may be required to show proof of residency that matches the address shown on this pass

➡ GO ON TO THE NEXT PAGE.

85. What information does the City of Redbank want to convey to residents?
    (A) Details of new waste disposal charges
    (B) How to dispose of some waste free of charge
    (C) The location of a new waste disposal facility
    (D) How to pay for waste disposal

86. Who can use the pass?
    (A) Any resident of the City of Redbank
    (B) Any business located in the City of Redbank
    (C) City waste disposal employees
    (D) The resident whose address is on the pass

87. What must a resident do if he or she does not have a pass when dumping waste?
    (A) Pay a fee
    (B) Apply for a new pass
    (C) Pay a fee and ask for a refund later
    (D) Register his or her name and address

Questions 88-90 refer to the following public announcement.

A new law for hybrid vehicles has become effective. If you buy a new hybrid vehicle by December 31, 2009, you may be eligible for a one-time federal income tax deduction of up to $2,000.

The amount of deduction will depend upon the vehicle's fuel economy, estimated fuel savings, and other factors.

For your vehicle to qualify for the tax deduction, the following requirements must also be met:

a. You must purchase the vehicle new and for your own use, not for resale.
b. You must drive it mostly in the United States.
c. The vehicle must meet all federal and state exhaust gas emissions requirements.
d. Government agencies, tax-exempt organizations, and foreign entities are not eligible.

Visit our website for updated tax credit information.

88. What benefit can people get if they buy a new hybrid car on December 15, 2009?
   (A) They can get $2,000 cash back.
   (B) They can have a maximum of $2,000 deducted from their taxable income.
   (C) They have until December 31 to pay the tax.
   (D) They can apply for a tax deduction at any time.

89. How will the amount of tax deduction be decided?
   (A) It will depend on the size of the car.
   (B) It will depend on the cost of the car.
   (C) It will depend on the gas mileage and energy savings.
   (D) It will be up to the tax office to decide.

90. What kind of hybrid car qualifies for a tax deduction?
   (A) One used by a foreign company
   (B) One imported from Japan
   (C) One bought new for personal use
   (D) One that is intended to be resold

➡ GO ON TO THE NEXT PAGE.

To: Frances Delmore
From: Roger Crawford
Subject: House to let

Dear Ms. Delmore,

I'm very interested in renting a house in the south of France in summer this year and I saw your advertisement for a house in that area. According to your brief description, it seems very suitable, but I would like to confirm a few points before making a definite offer. I would like to rent a house for the whole of July and August. I am in the process of writing a book and so I need a quiet house where I can concentrate. My wife is a painter, and so she will need a large room with south-facing windows so that she can get as much sunlight as possible. We also have young twin boys, who will share a bedroom. They love swimming, and so we would like to be near the sea – perhaps a 30-minute drive at most. As the house is in the countryside, I hope it will be no problem for us to bring our dog with us. I would be very grateful if you could e-mail me with your answers as soon as possible, because we would like to secure a rental property before it is too late.

Kind regards,

Roger Crawford

To: Roger Crawford
From: Frances Delmore
Subject: Re: House to let

Dear Mr. Crawford,

Many thanks for your message regarding my house in the south of France. It's a beautiful old farmhouse with a large kitchen, a lounge, a dining room, four bedrooms and two bathrooms. It also has a large garden. Let me answer the points you raised. The house and the surrounding area are very quiet and peaceful. The house actually stands at the edge of the village on a country road with very little traffic. The master bedroom is the largest, and faces south, and would be the best room for your wife to use as a studio. This means you and your wife would have to sleep in the second bedroom, but don't worry, because this is also quite large. The only problem is that the closest beach is about one-hour's drive away. However, there is a beautiful lake just ten-minutes' walk from the house. It is clean, safe and very popular with local families.

Dogs, of course, are no problem. However, I had some renters in the house once that brought cats with them. The cats caused such a lot of damage that I'm afraid those animals are no longer welcome! If you are still interested, please contact me as soon as possible.

Yours sincerely,
Frances Delmore

91. What is the relationship between Frances Delmore and Roger Crawford?
    (A) Frances Delmore owns the house Roger Crawford lives in.
    (B) Roger Crawford wants to buy Frances Delmore's house.
    (C) They are old friends.
    (D) They have never met each other.

92. What does Roger Crawford want to do in the summer?
    (A) Spend three months in the south of France.
    (B) Paint a picture of his wife.
    (C) Find a quiet place to write.
    (D) Have a vacation at the beach.

93. What problem does Frances Delmore mention?
    (A) There is nowhere for the boys to swim.
    (B) No room faces south.
    (C) The house is far away from the village.
    (D) Some pets are not allowed.

94. How many bedrooms will Roger Crawford's family likely use?
    (A) One
    (B) Two
    (C) Three
    (D) Four

95. In the first e-mail, the phrase "in the process of" in line 4, is closest in meaning to
    (A) in the middle of
    (B) about to finish
    (C) doing research for
    (D) having problems with

➡ GO ON TO THE NEXT PAGE.

TRY THE AMAZING PERMAWARM HEAT PADS!

Permawarm Heat Pads

- Last for 12 hours   - Ultra-light
                        - Odorless

Permawarm Heat Pads are perfect for those times when you need a steady supply of heat. Permawarm Heat Pads are thin and portable. Just place a heat pad over the part of your body that needs warmth. It will then heat up naturally to deliver up to 12 hours of continued warmth. Use them to ease sports injuries and muscle aches, or take them outdoors to any place where you'll feel the cold.

Permawarm Heat Pads for Feet

- Last for five hours   - Thin and comfortable
- Fits the shape of feet   - Anti-bacterial and deodorizing

Permawarm Heat Pads for Feet are designed to fit into men's and women's shoes when you want to keep your toes nice and warm. Use Permawarm Heat Pads for Feet when you're outside watching sports games, at outdoor events such as weddings or the races, or for outdoor pursuits such as skiing or fishing. Permawarm Heat Pads for Feet are designed not to slip when inside your shoes, and are also anti-bacterial and deodorizing.

For more information contact us at info@permawarm.com

To: info@permawarm.com
From: hnielsen@sol.com
Subject: Inquiry regarding Permawarm Heat Pads

I was browsing the Internet earlier today when I came across your site. My husband and I run a small company in Copenhagen. We've been in business for about two years, and the company now has a stable clients base in Denmark, Norway, Sweden and Finland. We deal mainly in fashion accessories for women, and I think your heated pads would be a very useful addition to our range of products.

The company is an Internet-based vendor—we sell only through our Web site, I would be very interested in finding out some more about your products. In addition, if sales are successful and we establish a good working relationship, could we discuss the possibility of becoming your exclusive distributor in Scandinavia at some point in the future?

I look forward very much to hearing from you. If you like, please check my company's Web site at www.allegria.co.dk for a look at our current product line.

Kind regards,
Hilde Nielsen
President

96. How many different products does
    Permawarm offer?
    (A) One
    (B) Two
    (C) Five
    (D) Twelve

97. What is NOT included in the features of
    Permawarm Heat Pads for Feet?
    (A) They keep your feet free of germs and
        bad smells.
    (B) They do not move around in your
        shoes.
    (C) They last for five hours.
    (D) They are waterproof.

98. What does Hilde Nielsen's company do?
    (A) It provides Internet service.
    (B) It sells goods in fashion stores.
    (C) It is a wholesale supplier.
    (D) It sells goods online.

99. Why is Hilde Nielsen interested in
    Permawarm's products?
    (A) They are cheap.
    (B) They go with her company's other
        products.
    (C) Scandinavia has cold winters.
    (D) Her husband recommended them.

100. What does Hilde Nielsen want her
    company to do in the future?
    (A) Start to manufacture heat pads.
    (B) Set up branches all over Scandinavia.
    (C) Become Permawarm's only
        Scandinavian importer.
    (D) Give up its current business and
        become a wholesaler.

**Stop! This is the end of the test. If you finish before time is called, you may go
back to Parts 5, 6, and 7 and check your work.**

Full Test

200 題

LISTENING TEST （ p. 82-96）45 分鐘
READING TEST 　（ p. 97-127）把計時器設定為 75 分鐘。

LISTENING TEST 的 ◎ mp3 音軌從 Track 51 開始播放。

LISTENING TEST

In the Listening test, your will be asked to demonstrate how well you understand spoken English. The entire Listening test will last approximately 45 minutes. There are four parts, and directions are given for each part. You must mark your answers on the separate answer sheet. Do not write your answers in your test book.

Part 1

Directions: For each question in this part, you will hear four statements about a picture in your test book. When you hear the statements, you must select the one statement that best describes what you see in the picture. Then find the number of the question on your answer sheet and mark your answer. The statements will be printed in your test book and will be spoken only one time.

Example   Sample Answer

Statement (C), "They're standing near the table," is the best description of the picture, so you should select answer (C) and mark it on your answer sheet.

1.

2.

➡ *GO ON TO THE NEXT PAGE.*

3.

4.

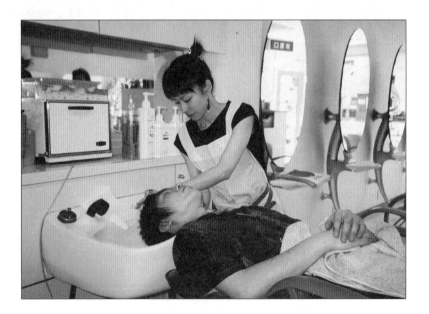

5.

6.

➡ *GO ON TO THE NEXT PAGE.*

7.

8.

9.

10.

➡ *GO ON TO THE NEXT PAGE.*

Part 2

Directions: You will hear a question or statement and three responses spoken in English. They will not be printed in your test book and will be spoken only one time. Select the best response to the question or statement and mark the letter (A), (B), or (C) on your answer sheet.

Example

Sample Answer
Ⓐ ● Ⓒ

You will hear: Where is the meeting room?

You will also hear: (A) To meet the new director.
                        (B) It's the first room on the right.
                        (C) Yes, at two o'clock.

The best response to the question "Where is the meeting room?" is choice (B), "It's the first room on the right," so (B) is the correct answer. You should mark answer (B) on your answer sheet.

11. Mark your answer on your answer sheet.

12. Mark your answer on your answer sheet.

13. Mark your answer on your answer sheet.

14. Mark your answer on your answer sheet.

15. Mark your answer on your answer sheet.

16. Mark your answer on your answer sheet.

17. Mark your answer on your answer sheet.

18. Mark your answer on your answer sheet.

19. Mark your answer on your answer sheet.

20. Mark your answer on your answer sheet.

21. Mark your answer on your answer sheet.

22. Mark your answer on your answer sheet.

23. Mark your answer on your answer sheet.

24. Mark your answer on your answer sheet.

25. Mark your answer on your answer sheet.

26. Mark your answer on your answer sheet.

27. Mark your answer on your answer sheet.

28. Mark your answer on your answer sheet.

29. Mark your answer on your answer sheet.

30. Mark your answer on your answer sheet.

31. Mark your answer on your answer sheet.

32. Mark your answer on your answer sheet.

33. Mark your answer on your answer sheet.

34. Mark your answer on your answer sheet.

35. Mark your answer on your answer sheet.

36. Mark your answer on your answer sheet.

37. Mark your answer on your answer sheet.

38. Mark your answer on your answer sheet.

39. Mark your answer on your answer sheet.

40. Mark your answer on your answer sheet.

Part 3

Directions: You will hear some conversations between two people. You will be asked to answer three questions about what the speakers say in each conversation. Select the best response to each question and mark the letter (A), (B), (C), or (D) on your answer sheet. The conversations will not be printed in your test book and will be spoken only one time.

41. What is wrong with the man's car?
    (A) He needs to have a tire changed.
    (B) It's out of gas.
    (C) It's not running very well.
    (D) The oil needs to be changed.

42. When does he need the car?
    (A) Tomorrow
    (B) Until 5:00
    (C) By 5:00
    (D) When it's finished

43. What number did he give to the woman?
    (A) His work number
    (B) His home number
    (C) His mobile number
    (D) His license plate number

44. How many different items does the man have to order?
    (A) Two
    (B) Three
    (C) Four
    (D) Six

45. Which item do they need the soonest?
    (A) Paper
    (B) Salespeople
    (C) Batteries for their laptops
    (D) Toner cartridges

46. What does the woman say about the paper order?
    (A) It is okay to accept any size paper.
    (B) They need it as quickly as possible.
    (C) There is no rush.
    (D) They do not need paper for the copier.

➡ GO ON TO THE NEXT PAGE.

Pre Test

Half Test 1

Half Test 2

Full Test

47. What does the woman ask about?
    (A) Sending a cake as a gift
    (B) Having a cake delivered
    (C) Delivering a cake herself
    (D) Baking a cake herself

48. How will the woman get the cake?
    (A) She will deliver it.
    (B) She will have it delivered.
    (C) She will pick it up.
    (D) She will go to the suburbs.

49. Who is Einstein?
    (A) The woman
    (B) The man
    (C) The woman's son
    (D) The woman's cat

50. What does the front desk ask Mr. Jameson about?
    (A) When he made a reservation
    (B) How long he will stay
    (C) If his name is correct
    (D) If he has a credit card

51. What does Mr. Jameson want to do?
    (A) Change the room.
    (B) Stay for the night.
    (C) Pay with his credit card.
    (D) Cancel the reservation.

52. What did the clerk tell Mr. Jameson about his credit card?
    (A) The hotel does not accept credit cards.
    (B) The hotel accepts only bank credit cards.
    (C) The card has been accepted.
    (D) The card is no longer valid.

53. What is the woman looking for?
    (A) Her supervisor
    (B) Mr. Belmont's office
    (C) Advice about Mr. Belmont
    (D) The way to get to the fifth floor

54. What advice does the man give the woman?
    (A) To go straight down the hallway
    (B) Not to get angry
    (C) To knock on Mr. Belmont's door
    (D) To go to Mr. Belmont's office

55. What information does the man NOT give to the woman?
    (A) Directions to Mr. Belmont's office
    (B) Advice about knocking on Mr. Belmont's door
    (C) His relationship with Mr. Belmont
    (D) Where to take the elevator

56. What are the two people discussing?
    (A) A problem with the air conditioner
    (B) The maintenance department
    (C) The weather condition
    (D) Complaints from clients

57. When are the maintenance people supposed to come?
    (A) Right away
    (B) At 4 o'clock
    (C) After they finish the work on the 3rd floor
    (D) Not within today

58. What does the man suggest?
    (A) Forgetting about the problem
    (B) Calling maintenance again
    (C) Calling another company
    (D) Fixing the air conditioning by themselves

59. What is the woman's problem?
    (A) The usher is very rude to her.
    (B) Someone is sitting in her seat.
    (C) A large man stole her ticket.
    (D) The woman lost her ticket.

60. How did the man react when the woman showed him her ticket?
    (A) He apologized and moved to the next seat.
    (B) He didn't care what the woman said to him.
    (C) He showed his own ticket to prove he was right.
    (D) He yelled at her and told her to go away.

61. How is the usher probably going to help the woman?
    (A) He will persuade the big man to give up the seat.
    (B) He will call the police and report the incident.
    (C) He will give the big man a free ticket.
    (D) He will go to the big man and throw him out.

62. What does the man need to do next?
    (A) To get off the elevator at the 37th floor
    (B) To press the button for 37
    (C) To go downstairs and find the correct elevator
    (D) To go as high as the 24th floor

63. What does the woman tell him?
    (A) How to find the elevator he needs to use
    (B) How to find a security guard
    (C) How many floors there are in the building
    (D) How to get to the first floor

64. What should he do if he can't find the correct elevators?
    (A) Look at the map on the wall
    (B) Ask another passenger on the elevator
    (C) Go to the 37th floor
    (D) Ask someone who works in the building

65. What are they discussing?
    (A) Merchandise on sale
    (B) Exchanging an item
    (C) A lost receipt
    (D) A sweater returned a week ago

66. Why can't the customer exchange the sweater?
    (A) He does not have proof of purchase.
    (B) He bought it a week ago.
    (C) He bought it on sale.
    (D) He already wore it.

67. How does the customer feel about the store policy?
    (A) They should have tried it on.
    (B) They should give back the money.
    (C) They should have told him about the policy.
    (D) They should have warned about the size.

➡ GO ON TO THE NEXT PAGE.

68. What happened to the woman's contact lens?
    (A) It rolled off the desk.
    (B) It fell out of her purse.
    (C) She took it out and dropped it.
    (D) It came out of her eye.

69. Why does she think it will be difficult to find?
    (A) The color of the carpet is very light.
    (B) George won't help her find it.
    (C) She cannot drive without her contact lenses.
    (D) She could have dropped it somewhere else.

70. What does the woman tell George?
    (A) To go down and find an optical shop
    (B) To tell her where the lens is
    (C) To look for the white carpet
    (D) To be careful where he steps

Part 4

Directions: You will hear some talks given by a single speaker. You will be asked to answer three questions about what the speaker says in each talk. Select the best response to each question and mark the letter (A), (B), (C), or (D) on your answer sheet. The talks will not be printed in your test book and will be spoken only one time.

71. How can the caller speak with an airline representative?
    (A) By pressing 4
    (B) By pressing 5
    (C) By holding the line
    (D) By calling a different number

72. What number should the caller press to learn about the World Trotter mileage program?
    (A) 1
    (B) 2
    (C) 3
    (D) 4

73. How does the automated assistance system help the caller?
    (A) It is more pleasant than talking to the operator.
    (B) It helps the caller to get what they need quickly.
    (C) The operator answers each call politely.
    (D) Callers are given special discounts on tickets.

74. Why are some schools closing for the day?
    (A) A storm is coming.
    (B) A snowstorm came last night.
    (C) The school bus is not running.
    (D) All the roads are closed.

75. Which district is closing all of its schools?
    (A) Fairbright
    (B) Wesley Smith
    (C) Jefferson City
    (D) Taft Brentwood

76. What are parents expected to do?
    (A) Have their children leave home earlier.
    (B) Have their children stay home from school.
    (C) Drive their children to school.
    (D) Wait for the school bus to arrive.

GO ON TO THE NEXT PAGE.

77. What kind of program is "Empty Pages"?
    (A) A comedy
    (B) A mystery
    (C) A documentary
    (D) A family drama

78. What makes the comedy show featuring Dan and Stan so popular?
    (A) They have funny faces.
    (B) They are inventive.
    (C) They make stupid mistakes.
    (D) They always succeed in life.

79. What kind of people will we probably see if we watch Channel 7 at 9:00?
    (A) Lawyers
    (B) Librarian
    (C) Teachers
    (D) Businessperson

___

80. How long was the boy trapped underground?
    (A) Two days
    (B) Three days
    (C) Three nights
    (D) Overnight

81. What was the boy doing when he fell into the well?
    (A) He was cycling in the street.
    (B) He was playing in the garden.
    (C) He was walking in the tunnel.
    (D) He was working in the garage.

82. How was the boy's condition when he was rescued?
    (A) He was very tired but not hurt badly.
    (B) He was terrified and injured badly.
    (C) He was unconscious.
    (D) He was lively and talkative.

___

83. What are the three specials they offer?
    (A) Fish, pork and chicken
    (B) Fish, pasta and chicken
    (C) Fish, meat and pasta
    (D) Fish, salad and pasta

84. What kind of meat dish is offered on the special menu?
    (A) Beefsteak
    (B) Pork cutlet
    (C) Roast chicken
    (D) Lamb roast

85. How late is the restaurant open?
    (A) As long as there are customers
    (B) As long as the food lasts
    (C) Until 12:00
    (D) Until 11:00

___

86. Where is this talk being given?
    (A) At a school
    (B) At a restaurant
    (C) At a hospital
    (D) At a company office

87. What happened to two employees?
    (A) They caught a virus.
    (B) Their data was stolen.
    (C) Their data was lost.
    (D) Their hard disks were replaced.

88. What should the employees NOT do?
    (A) Share their personal passwords.
    (B) Open e-mail.
    (C) Leave their desks.
    (D) Visit websites.

___

89. What type of event is taking place?
    (A) A security inspection
    (B) A play
    (C) A baseball game
    (D) A concert

90. What items cannot be brought into the stadium?
    (A) Knapsacks and alcoholic beverages
    (B) Cameras and shoulder bags
    (C) Cameras and alcoholic beverages
    (D) Alcoholic beverages and tickets

91. What will happen to cameras if they are found during inspection?
    (A) The inspector will take the person's picture.
    (B) The inspector will take the camera, and return it after the event.
    (C) The inspector will take the camera and not return it.
    (D) The inspector will take out the film and keep it.

92. What is the purpose of the compact disc?
    (A) To thank the customer
    (B) To tell the customer how to set up the stereo
    (C) To sell the customer a subwoofer
    (D) To make sure no parts are missing

93. Where must the control amplifier be positioned?
    (A) On the bottom
    (B) In a stack
    (C) On top of the other components
    (D) In the box

94. Who should continue to listen to the compact disc?
    (A) People who didn't understand the instructions
    (B) People who like to listen to music
    (C) People who have stereo systems
    (D) People who bought the system with the subwoofer

95. What is on sale with blue tags?
    (A) Canned goods
    (B) Frozen foods
    (C) All the dairy products
    (D) Fruits and vegetables

96. How many canned products on sale can a customer buy?
    (A) As many as they want
    (B) Up to six per customer
    (C) Up to five per customer
    (D) One can for every two cans

97. How can customers get a 5% discount at the cash register?
    (A) By showing the discount items they bought
    (B) By showing identification
    (C) By showing their member's card
    (D) By shopping before noon

➡ GO ON TO THE NEXT PAGE.

98. Who is the speaker?
    (A) The coach of Westmore State
    (B) The coach of the losing team
    (C) A reporter
    (D) A player on the winning team

99. Why does the speaker think the team lost?
    (A) They didn't want to win the game badly enough.
    (B) They were better than the other team.
    (C) Their best players were injured.
    (D) Their best players were healthy.

100. What did the speaker say about Westmore State?
    (A) They looked hungry.
    (B) They were in the locker room.
    (C) They were worthy champions.
    (D) They were playing better than ever.

READING TEST

In the Reading test, you will read a variety of texts and answer several different types of reading comprehension questions. The entire Reading test will last 75 minutes. There are three parts, and directions are given for each part. You are encouraged to answer as many questions as possible within the time allowed.

You must mark your answers on the separate answer sheet. Do not write your answers in your test book.

Part 5

Directions: A word or phrase is missing in each of the sentences below. Four answer choices are given below each sentence. Select the best answer to complete the sentence. Then mark the letter (A), (B), (C), or (D) on your answer sheet.

Pre Test

Half Test 1

Half Test 2

Full Test

101. Could you make ------- for me? I'd like to sit down.
(A) room
(B) rooms
(C) a room
(D) roomy

102. The order ------- yesterday will be shipped by global priority mail.
(A) placed
(B) put
(C) given
(D) done

103. I ------- better than to invest all my money in the new start-up business last year.
(A) know
(B) have known
(C) should know
(D) should have known

104. The only problem with my new camera is that it does not have ------- batteries.
(A) recharge
(B) recharger
(C) recharging
(D) rechargeable

105. Fortunately, Monday's earthquake did not ------- any significant damage.
(A) do
(B) trouble
(C) suffer
(D) give

106. Applicants must be 18 years old or above to take ------- in the competition.
(A) place
(B) part
(C) sides
(D) over

107. In ------- to the downsizing trend in the market, the firm recruited extra staff.
(A) contrary
(B) contrast
(C) compare
(D) conflict

108. ------- the sudden increase in customers, we may achieve our goal much earlier than we expected.
(A) With
(B) From
(C) By
(D) As

➡ GO ON TO THE NEXT PAGE.

109. The downturn in the economy is making it much harder for new graduates to ------- jobs.
(A) security
(B) secure
(C) securing
(D) secured

110. This software application is ------- for the average user.
(A) complication
(B) complicated
(C) complicate
(D) complicating

111. The survey showed that fewer than half the employees were in ------- of adopting flextime working hours.
(A) favor
(B) favored
(C) favorable
(D) favoring

112. The new filing system will ------- us a lot of time and trouble in finding the right folder.
(A) stop
(B) prevent
(C) end
(D) save

113. The CEO will make ------- about the new models at the conference in San Diego next week.
(A) announce
(B) announcing
(C) an announcement
(D) an announcer

114. The information provided in these reports is ------- for in-house use only.
(A) intent
(B) intended
(C) intending
(D) intention

115. Rival firms have grown ------- at our activities in this area that they have united against us.
(A) so alarmed
(B) so alarming
(C) too alarming
(D) too alarmed

116. This area has a less humid climate than ------- other in the country, and is perfect for growing grapes.
(A) any
(B) some
(C) all
(D) most

117. The key to ------- good decisions for your business is to know all available options.
(A) make
(B) made
(C) have made
(D) making

118. This DVD player is so hard to operate that I have spent twice ------- time reading the manual as using the machine itself.
(A) more
(B) most
(C) as much
(D) as many

119. ------- the customers seem to be very pleased with the company's level of service.
(A) Most of
(B) Mostly
(C) Almost
(D) Any of

120. Every candidate must have ------- of electronics and a valid work visa.
(A) knowledge enough
(B) a good knowledge
(C) well knowing
(D) known well

121. Who do you think the best soccer player
------- this year?
(A) be
(B) been
(C) was
(D) had been

122. The old manual typewriter in the display
case ------- me of the early days of the
company.
(A) remembers
(B) memorizes
(C) reminds
(D) recalls

123. If it ------- for your advice, we could never
have met the deadline.
(A) had not been
(B) would not be
(C) is not for
(D) will not be

124. The Stark Foundation's new residential
development ------- five units of single-
parent family homes.
(A) consisting of
(B) consists of
(C) is consisted by
(D) was consisted

125. Avoid incorrect punctuation and -------
used capital letters because this may
confuse readers.
(A) inadequate
(B) bad
(C) wrongly
(D) properly

126. I have arranged a meeting ------- lunch
with our design director.
(A) for
(B) in
(C) while
(D) over

127. Before the 19th century, almost all
countries had to concentrate ------- the
task of feeding their people.
(A) for
(B) in
(C) over
(D) on

128. James, Katherine and Terry are going to
play the parts of the husband, the wife
and her lover ------- in the next musical.
(A) respectfully
(B) respectable
(C) respective
(D) respectively

129. The company's range of products
includes semiconductors, ------- and
petrochemicals.
(A) heavy equipment
(B) heavy equipments
(C) heavily equipment
(D) heavily equipments

130. Ms. Schultz ------- leaving for London
tomorrow morning, but she can be
reached at this number.
(A) be
(B) will be
(C) was
(D) would be

131. The latest report shows that these books
published last month are ------- very well.
(A) selling
(B) sold
(C) being sold
(D) sales

➡ GO ON TO THE NEXT PAGE.

Pre Test

Half Test 1

Half Test 2

Full Test

132. In the U.S. you are ------- for a tax
deduction if you donate to a charity
organization certified by the government.
(A) liable
(B) credible
(C) eligible
(D) reliable

133. Their new office was completely
refurnished at ------- cost.
(A) great
(B) greatly
(C) most
(D) a few

134. The customer service department -------
the client that he had to show in what
way the product was defective.
(A) said
(B) spoke
(C) talked
(D) told

135. ------- employees who want to use these
facilities must attend an orientation
session.
(A) Most
(B) Some
(C) All
(D) Every

136. Temporary staff ------- after in-patients at
our hospital are usually paid 15 dollars
an hour plus transportation expenses.
(A) look
(B) looked
(C) was looking
(D) looking

137. There were many inquiries about when
operations at the plant -------.
(A) resume
(B) be resumed
(C) resuming
(D) would resume

138. Imprecise use of language can -------
confusion and misinterpretation in
business deals.
(A) result from
(B) come across
(C) take up
(D) lead to

139. By law, all employees and visitors -------
wear hard hats when entering the
construction site.
(A) can
(B) might
(C) must
(D) should

140. Full-time ------- who have worked for the
company for 12 months are entitled to
two weeks' paid vacation.
(A) employment
(B) employees
(C) employers
(D) employed

Part 6

Directions: Read the texts that follow. A word or phrase is missing in some of the sentences. Four answer choices are given below each of the sentences. Select the best answer to complete the text. Then mark the letter (A), (B), (C), or (D) on your answer sheet.

Questions 141-143 refer to the following message.

An important message to our customers

Recently there has been a huge increase in Internet fraud, and many people have been tricked into ------- personal information, such as bank account numbers and passwords.

    141. (A) creating
         (B) opening
         (C) stealing
         (D) revealing

If you log on to our Web site and are directed to a page you have never seen before, please read the page ------- before you enter any information. If you are asked to reconfirm your

    142. (A) care
         (B) caring
         (C) careful
         (D) carefully

account numbers, passwords or any other personal information, do not do so ------- you have

    143. (A) after
         (B) since
         (C) until
         (D) while

confirmed that the page is genuine.

If you have any doubts, go to our home page, or call our customer service department at 1-800-754-0011.

➡ GO ON TO THE NEXT PAGE.

Mr. Gerard Fenton
357 Marriot Street
Harrisburg PA 17101

Dear Mr. Fenton,

Thank you for your recent ------- for a housing loan. However, we need some more

144. (A) apply
(B) applicant
(C) appliance
(D) application

information from you concerning your current income before we can process your application.

We would like you to send us two recent pay slips as well as a letter from your current -------

145. (A) employ
(B) employer
(C) employee
(D) employment

with details of your annual salary.

Payment for the property is due on July 31, so we need to act quickly if we are to meet the deadline. If you have any questions, please don't hesitate to get ------- touch with me.

146. (A) in
(B) at
(C) on
(D) by

You can contact me by e-mail at karenb@ghsbanking.com, or call me at 6539-7001 direct.

I look forward to hearing from you soon.

Sincerely,

Karen Berger

Karen Berger
Customer Relations Manager

Questions 147-149 refer to the following want ad.

INTERNSHIP AVAILABLE IN THE MUSIC INDUSTRY

Argus Music, a well-established artist management agency, is looking for an enthusiastic young person to work as an intern. ------- will include general office administration work,

147. (A) Response
(B) Responsible
(C) Responsibilities
(D) Responsive

answering telephone calls and keeping production information up to date.

You will also occasionally be expected to accompany artists to recording studios to -------

148. (A) show
(B) illustrate
(C) represent
(D) demonstrate

the company and deal with any possible problems.

This is an ideal opportunity for an energetic and motivated young person to develop skills and knowledge that will prove ------- toward a future career in the entertainment industry.

149. (A) worthless
(B) invaluable
(C) inexpensive
(D) pointless

After six months of internship, we may consider the intern for a paid position on the staff if the intern's performance has been of a sufficiently high standard.

If you are well-organized, have good people skills and are looking for a springboard to a career in a stimulating and vibrant industry, contact us for an interview.

➡ GO ON TO THE NEXT PAGE.

Pre Test

Half Test 1

Half Test 2

Full Test

Questions 150-152 refer to the following notice.

ALBANY ANTIQUES AND FINE ART FAIR: CANCELLATION NOTICE

We regret to announce the cancellation of this year's Albany Antiques and Fine Art Fair, one of the country's best-known art and antiques fairs. This year's event was scheduled to run from September 3 to 8 at the Harold Jacobson Conference Center. Unfortunately, ------- a serious

150. (A) because
(B) resulting from
(C) in spite of
(D) with respect to

fire, the place is no longer available. It was very badly damaged and it is now completely out of the ------- to use it.

151. (A) picture
(B) question
(C) possibility
(D) planning

Naturally, we have made great efforts to find an alternative site, but it is now already July, and all other suitable sites in the area are booked. We offer our sincere apologies to all the dealers who have already reserved space at the fair. We will provide a full refund of all the rental fees you have paid, along ------- a 10% discount on next year's fees.

152. (A) for
(B) with
(C) to
(D) together

We look forward to welcoming you at next year's fair. For further details, please contact our Customer Services Manager, Jennifer Benson, at jbenson@aafaf.com.

Part 7

Directions: In this part you will read a selection of texts, such as magazine and newspaper articles, letters and advertisements. Each text is followed by several questions. Select the best answer for each question and mark the letter (A), (B), (C), or (D) on your answer sheet.

Questions 153-154 refer to the following e-mail.

Date: April 24, 2009
To: All staff
From: Tom Nolan, IT Manager
Subject: Virus Protection

As you all know, we have had some problems recently with viruses infecting some of our office computers. This has caused some serious problems with loss of data, and the company has lost a large number of working hours because it took a long time to remove these viruses. Last December, the IT Department sent instructions to all staff on how to avoid getting viruses in your computers. I earnestly ask all of you to read this again and make sure you are taking all necessary care. One piece of advice I must repeat is this: Do NOT open any e-mail attachment unless you are absolutely certain of what it is and who sent it to you. Also, in order to increase our protection, we have recently purchased the most up-to-date virus protection software. From Monday through Friday next week, members of the IT department will be installing it in every computer in the company. The schedule is posted on the company bulletin board, so please refer to this. While this new software is being installed, you will not be able to use your own computer. So please make sure that you copy all your important data onto an external hard drive so that you can use it on a separate computer if necessary.

Tom Nolan
IT Manager

153. What is the purpose of this message?
(A) To warn staff about a new kind of computer virus
(B) To give detailed instructions on how to get rid of computer virus
(C) To inform staff about installing new software
(D) To inform staff about installing new computers

154. What problem will staff have in the following week?
(A) They will not be able to open e-mail attachments.
(B) They will have to search for computer viruses.
(C) Their computers will be replaced with new ones.
(D) Their computers will not be available temporarily.

➡ GO ON TO THE NEXT PAGE.

Work abroad this summer
at Hotel Tropicana!

- Free accommodation
- Full board
- Varied work

Qualifications:

Applicants must possess proper visas and should have sufficient communication skills in English. Experience in hotel work is an advantage but is not essential.

Conditions:

- Employees will have one free day per week, which can be any day except Saturday and Sunday.
- Employees are expected to look neat and tidy at all times. The hotel is responsible for cleaning employee uniforms, which the hotel provides.
- All facilities in our hotel such as tennis courts, gym, pool and beauty salon are available to employees outside duty hours. Charges for use will be 60 percent of normal fees.

155. What is one of the benefits for workers at the hotel?
    (A) They do not have to pay for meals.
    (B) They are allowed free use of all the facilities.
    (C) They can choose any work they like.
    (D) They have to buy their own work clothes.

156. What is one requirement for job applicants?
    (A) They should speak English and one other language.
    (B) They should have experience in hotel work.
    (C) They must have a work visa.
    (D) They must be in their early 20s.

157. Which condition does NOT apply to the employees?
    (A) They can take a day off on any day but weekends.
    (B) They can use the gym free of charge.
    (C) They are not expected to clean their uniforms.
    (D) They must be careful about their appearance.

➡ *GO ON TO THE NEXT PAGE.*

Safety Standards Division
321 Orange Street, West Lafayette IN 47695

Mr. Francis Grainger
438 West Beasdale Street
Purdue IN 47597

June 3, 2009

Dear Mr. Grainger:

The Safety Standards Division (SSD) has conducted a sidewalk inspection and has noted that the sidewalks in front of your house cannot be considered to be safe according to their standards. These defects could cause people to trip and fall. According to state law, every landowner is responsible for keeping his or her sidewalks in good repair. Some sidewalks can be repaired by grinding down the affected area, but in some cases they may need more overall repairs.

Every owner who receives this notice and whose sidewalks need repairing must complete the work by November 30 of this year. You must obtain a permit before the repairs can begin. Permits are available free of charge at the headquarters of the Safety Standards Division, 321 Orange Street. After the work has been completed, please call your nearest SSD office to arrange for an inspection.

If you have any questions or desire more information, please call SSD headquarters at 217-236-8659.

Sincerely,

Louise D. Scully

Louise D. Scully
Safety Standards Director

158. What does the Safety Standards Division
     tell Mr. Grainger?
     (A) It plans to arrange a sidewalk
         inspection.
     (B) It wants him to come to the office for
         an interview.
     (C) It wants him to repair his sidewalks.
     (D) It will repair defective sidewalks.

159. What does Mr. Grainger have to do?
     (A) Obtain a permit for the SSD to repair
         the sidewalks.
     (B) Start to repair his sidewalks by
         November 30.
     (C) Finish his sidewalk repairs by
         November 30.
     (D) Begin sidewalk repairs before
         getting a permit.

160. Where does the SSD issue permits for
     sidewalk repairs?
     (A) At its main office
     (B) On West Beasdale Street
     (C) At the landowner's nearest SSD
         office
     (D) At the inspection site

161. What does Mr. Grainger have to do after
     repairs are completed?
     (A) Apply for a permit every year.
     (B) Have his sidewalk repair inspected.
     (C) Pay for the repair at the SSD office.
     (D) Inspect the sidewalk himself.

➡ *GO ON TO THE NEXT PAGE.*

Pre Test

Half Test 1

Half Test 2

Full Test

Ms. Dorothy Garland
Sales Manager
CE Engineering
425 Devon Industrial Park
West Edmonds WA 98026-6509

August 15, 2008

Dear Ms. Garland,

Since 1995, we have bought several printing machines and other necessary accessories from your company and have been satisfied with their performance. Recently, however, the quality of your after-sales service has become worse.

We installed two of your model-550B printers in 2005, and your regular twice-yearly service kept them in good working order. Whenever there was a breakdown, your service engineers would come to our factory within 24 hours.

However, last week, one of the printers stopped suddenly, so we called to request a visit from one of your agents. We expected him to come immediately, but he said the soonest he could arrange a visit would be in about seven days!

To make matters worse, the service engineer was supposed to arrive at 11 a.m., but he did not show up until after 4 p.m. Some of our engineers had to stay late until your agent had finished the repairs.

I am sure you can understand our dissatisfaction. We have already made a complaint about this incident to the service agent, but have not yet received any response.

We look forward to hearing from you and hope that you can promise an immediate improvement in your after-sales service.

Sincerely yours,

Dan Edwards

Dan Edwards
Production Manager
Trot Printing Service, Inc.

162. Why is the printing company dissatisfied with CE Engineering?
    (A) The quality of its machines is going down.
    (B) It cannot provide suitable machines.
    (C) Its engineers are not as skillful as before.
    (D) Its level of service has declined.

163. How often did a CE service engineer visit Trot Printing Service, Inc. in the past?
    (A) Once a year
    (B) Twice a year
    (C) Six times a year
    (D) Every month

164. What happened last week?
    (A) A machine broke down.
    (B) A machi ne was not delivered on time.
    (C) An engineer failed to repair a machine.
    (D) An engineer came a day late.

165. Why did Mr. Edwards write to Ms. Garland?
    (A) To sign a contract with her company
    (B) To build a better relationship with her
    (C) To ask for better service
    (D) To arrange a meeting

➡ GO ON TO THE NEXT PAGE.

How to Treat a Snakebite

Poisonous snakebites are medical emergencies and can be deadly. But they may not have serious effects if properly treated. So, the top priority is getting the victim to an emergency room as quickly as possible. However, before this, there are other things you can do to help.

Be sure to follow these rules

1. Keep the person calm. Movement helps the poison to spread. Try to keep the affected area below heart level to reduce the flow of poison.

2. Tie something (e.g. a handkerchief) tightly above the affected area to prevent the poison from spreading. If you have a pump-suction device, follow the manufacturer's directions.

Note: **DO NOT** suck the poison out using your mouth.

3. Be careful of the dead snake because it can bite as a reflex action for up to an hour after it is dead.

166. How should people be treated if they
   have been bitten by a poisonous snake?
   (A) They should be moved to a bed or a
   chair.
   (B) They should be taken to an
   emergency room as soon as
   possible.
   (C) The bite must be cleaned.
   (D) The bite should be bandaged.

167. Why is it important to keep the bite
   below heart level?
   (A) To keep the person calm
   (B) To stop the poison from spreading
   (C) To increase the flow of poison
   (D) To affect the area that was bitten

168. What should people do if they find a
   dead poisonous snake?
   (A) Take it to the doctor within an hour.
   (B) Check its reflexes.
   (C) Put it in a box.
   (D) Make sure not to touch it.

➡ *GO ON TO THE NEXT PAGE.*

Cleanmaster

Specialists in Carpet and Upholstery Cleaning

Major manufacturers recommend that carpets be professionally cleaned every 12 to 18 months and furnishings every 18 to 24 months to maintain their appearance. We can keep your carpets and furnishings looking their best with regular maintenance.

Upholstery Cleaning

Upholstery can be cleaned by steam, foam, or dry cleaning. Special attention must be given when cleaning upholstery. Carpet cleaning products should not be used for upholstery as it may contain fibers that require a different type of cleaner. With correct and regular care, upholstered furnishings will last for many years.

Oriental Rug Cleaning

Hand-Washing

We will remove dry loose soil and then use a special cleanser to loosen dirt and oils. We gently and thoroughly hand wash and rinse your delicate rug with our special cleaning solution. Any spots on your rug are carefully taken out with spot removers. The rug is then rinsed again to take out any remaining spot removers.

Dry Cleaning

We use our own dry cleaning product, which is specially prepared to clean natural fibers found in oriental rugs. The product will loosen the soils and leave the fibers soft without harming the dyes. Any spots on the rug are carefully taken out using spot removers.

*Your rug is picked up and delivered at no additional charge.

169. How often do manufacturers recommend furnishing be cleaned at least?
    (A) Twice a year
    (B) Every two years
    (C) Every two and a half years
    (D) Every three years

170. Why can upholstery furniture not be cleaned in the same way as carpets?
    (A) Carpet cleaners are too strong.
    (B) Carpet cleaners are too weak.
    (C) Upholstery may contain the same fibers as carpets.
    (D) Upholstery may contain different fibers than carpets.

171. What is done first if an oriental rug is washed by hand?
    (A) It is steam cleaned.
    (B) It is cleaned of dry soil.
    (C) Dirt and oil are loosened.
    (D) Spots are removed.

172. What should NOT be done to the carpet in the dry cleaning process?
    (A) Loosen dirt.
    (B) Remove spots.
    (C) Change the colors.
    (D) Make the fibers soft.

➡ GO ON TO THE NEXT PAGE.

Questions 173-176 refer to the following city guide.

DISCOVER LOS ANGELES

Los Angeles can be a difficult city to get around. It is so vast and sprawling that many tourists decide they have seen enough once they have visited Hollywood Boulevard or Universal Studios. But the City of Angels has a lot more to offer to those willing to make a little more effort — museums, music and perhaps the most diverse range of cuisines in the world. The biggest problem is getting around. The best idea is to hire a driver for the day, or prebook a taxi. Trying to flag down a taxi on the street is not easy, and navigating LA's complex freeway system is best taken care of by a driver already familiar with the city.

Perhaps the most famous of LA's cultural landmarks, the open-air Hollywood Bowl, is the place to go for a great musical experience, whether you like classical, rock, Latin American or any other kind of music. In this 18,000-seater arena, you can choose high-end seats at the front (usually requiring advance booking) or last-minute seats in the back for as little as a couple of dollars. Another place to hear great music is the Walt Disney Concert Hall, home of the Los Angeles Philharmonic. This hall is said to be among the most acoustically sophisticated concert halls in the world.

Two of the best art museums are the J. Paul Getty Museum and the Los Angeles County Museum of Art. "The Getty," as it is popularly known, has such impressive buildings and views that the buildings themselves are more famous than the collection of artworks inside. The County Museum has a fantastic collection of American, Asian and Islamic art, an ongoing film and music series, as well as touring exhibitions. There is free admission after 5 p.m. and on the second Tuesday of every month.

173. Why is Los Angeles a difficult city for tourists?
   (A) It is not easy to catch a taxi.
   (B) It has a high level of crime.
   (C) Transportation is very expensive.
   (D) It is hard to get from one place to another.

174. What is the best way to see the sights of Los Angeles?
   (A) Take a bus tour.
   (B) Hire an experienced driver.
   (C) Get a good map of the freeway system.
   (D) Plan the tour very carefully.

175. Which of the followings can be best appreciated from the outside?
   (A) The Hollywood Bowl
   (B) The Walt Disney Concert Hall
   (C) The J. Paul Getty Museum
   (D) The Los Angeles County Museum of Art

176. What is NOT a feature of the Hollywood Bowl?
   (A) It presents various styles of music.
   (B) Seats can be reserved at short notice.
   (C) The arena is uncovered.
   (D) It sometimes puts on free concerts.

➡ GO ON TO THE NEXT PAGE.

Don't stay in the dark!
Let GLOBAL BUSINESS JOURNAL
open your eyes to a world of opportunity

Get **Global Business Journal** delivered to your home for only $4.75 an issue!

Just fill out the attached form and return it with your payment using the envelope provided.

Get 12 issues annually for only $47.00!

PLEASE CHECK THE APPROPRIATE BOX BELOW:

□ **I WISH TO SUBSCRIBE to Global Business Journal.** I will continue my subscription each year unless I notify you otherwise. I understand I will continue to be billed annually at the prevailing rate.

Name: _____

Address:_____

_____

□ **SEND A GIFT SUBSCRIPTION** to the person named below.

Name: _____

Address:_____

_____

Payment method:

□ Personal check or □ international money order in U.S. funds enclosed for $_____

□ Charge my □ VISA □ MasterCard □ Diners Club □ American Express

*Credit card accounts will be charged in local currency at the rate of exchange applicable on the transaction date.

177. What is *Global Business Journal*?
     (A) A daily paper
     (B) A weekly magazine
     (C) A monthly magazine
     (D) An annual journal

178. What will happen if people do not inform
     the office they want to cancel their
     subscription?
     (A) No more copies will be delivered.
     (B) They will continue to receive issues.
     (C) They will be asked if they want to
         continue.
     (D) They will be notified that their
         subscription has expired.

179. What must people do to buy a
     subscription for a friend?
     (A) Get a gift card and send it to the
         friend directly.
     (B) Write the friend's name and address
         on the form.
     (C) Write their own name and address
         on the form.
     (D) Write the friend' s name and address
         as well as their own.

180. What kind of payment is NOT accepted?
     (A) Cash
     (B) Credit card
     (C) Personal check
     (D) International money order

➡ *GO ON TO THE NEXT PAGE.*

Pre Test

Half Test 1

Half Test 2

Full Test

Questions 181-185 refer to the following announcement and e-mail message.

BIANNUAL CHARITY DINNER FOR "HELP THE CHILDREN INTERNATIONAL"

Help the Children International is pleased to announce its upcoming charity dinner. The money we raise will help provide homeless children with shelter and education in countries all over the world. The dinner will be held at the Castle Hotel on November 15 from 7:00 p.m. to 11:00 p.m. Tickets are $75.00 per person. If you would like to attend, please follow the procedure outlined below.

How to make a reservation

1. For reservations, contact Nicola Spicer either by fax (756-9584-9955) or by e-mail (nspicer@htci.org). We are sorry but we cannot accept telephone reservations.
2. Closing date for reservations: Thursday, October 31.
3. Send payment by bank transfer to:
   Commercial Bank, Main Street Branch
   Account number: 1409383
   Account name: HTCI
4. Reservations are not considered accepted until payment is made.
5. Tables will seat 10 people. If your party is smaller, we will make the necessary arrangements for your group to share a table.
6. When reserving a table, please reserve and pay as a group, nominating a table leader, and providing a list of members in the party.

To: nspicer@htci.org
From: jholland@iol.com
Subject: Charity Dinner Reservations

Dear Nicola,

I'd like to make a booking for the Charity Dinner. I apologize for missing the deadline for reservations, but I've been out of the country for a while and have only just returned. I would be really grateful if you could still arrange for us to attend.
There will be six people in our party, and so I'd like to reserve a six-person table.
As soon as I know if it's still possible to make a reservation, I'll send the money by bank transfer and fax you the payment receipt.

Kind regards,
Jerry Holland
Group Leader

181. How often is the dinner held?
     (A) Every month
     (B) Every six months
     (C) Every year
     (D) Every other year

182. When will the organization officially
     accept a reservation?
     (A) When it receives cash from an
         applicant
     (B) When it receives a reservation form
     (C) When it receives payment into the
         bank account
     (D) When it receives an e-mail message

183. What kind of information is necessary to
     complete Jerry Holland's reservation?
     (A) The ages of the people in his group
     (B) The names of the people in his
         group
     (C) The name of his bank
     (D) His occupation

184. Which part of the instructions has Jerry
     Holland NOT understood?
     (A) The deadline for reservations
     (B) The number of people who can sit at
         one table
     (C) How to send confirmation of payment
     (D) The date of the charity dinner

185. How will the charity money be spent?
     (A) To train group leaders
     (B) To send volunteers to different
         countries
     (C) To provide children with food
     (D) To provide children with homes and
         schools

➡ GO ON TO THE NEXT PAGE.

Questions 186-190 refer to the following two letters.

Mr. James Cooper
Cooper Investment Services
Suite 4, Broadbent Tower
Independence Avenue
Pittsburgh PA 15204

Dear James,

How are you? I hope business is going well. As you are aware, I'm very grateful for the investment advice you've given me over the years we've known each other, and I was wondering if you might be able to help me again.

Like many other people, I've been rather disappointed with the performance of the stock market over the past couple of years, and I would like to try moving into a different area. I've seen many newspaper and magazine articles recently saying that it's a good time to invest in Australian real estate. Do you know of any good opportunities? If you do, I'd greatly appreciate your sending me some information.

Look forward to hearing from you.

Sincerely,

Kevin Miller
Kevin Miller

Mr. Kevin Miller
437 Greentree Blvd.
Harrisburg PA 17101

Dear Kevin,

It was good to hear from you after such a long time. I'd be very happy to help you in your search for a good real estate investment opportunity. There is certainly a lot of interest in the Australian market at present, and there are many new construction projects. We have done extensive research into new projects, and have finally decided on what we consider the best one. You can read the details of it below. Let me know if you're interested, and don't hesitate to get in touch if you have any questions.

Sincerely,

James Cooper
James Cooper

Sunrise City, Brisbane: A high-quality boutique apartment complex offering one- or two-bedroom luxury units, all with large terraces or gardens. Priced from $300,000 and up. Sunrise City is a high-end condominium situated very close to Brisbane's business district, but surrounded by landscaped parkland. Sunrise City also has a health club, an Olympic-size swimming pool, and child-care and pet-care facilities. The rental market is excellent, and there are very good prospects for capital growth.

186. What is the relationship between James
    Cooper and Kevin Miller?
    (A) Friends
    (B) Colleagues
    (C) Advisor and client
    (D) Superior and subordinate

187. Why did Kevin Miller write to James
    Cooper?
    (A) To sell some real estate
    (B) To get advice on an investment
    (C) To apply for a job
    (D) To carry out research

188. What is one benefit of buying an
    apartment in Sunrise City?
    (A) The price is very low.
    (B) The value is likely to rise.
    (C) Sunrise City is close to the beach.
    (D) The apartments have many
        bedrooms.

189. How long have Kevin Miller and James
    Cooper known each other?
    (A) This is their first communication.
    (B) A few weeks.
    (C) A few months.
    (D) A few years.

190. Who might be most interested in
    purchasing a condominium in Sunrise
    City?
    (A) A single person with low income
    (B) A retired senior citizen
    (C) A family with many children
    (D) A young working couple with a child

➡ GO ON TO THE NEXT PAGE.

Customer Service Manager
FRB Electronics
376 Flinders Plaza
Brisbane, QLD 4000

October 19

Dear Sir/Madam:

On August 10 I purchased an MW2000 toaster, one of your products for $85. This price included a 30-day money-back trial offer. The $85 was charged to my credit card. However, the first time I tried to use the toaster, I discovered the timer was defective, and on September 10, I decided to return it to your company. One of your staff informed me by phone that shipping and handling charges as well as the price of the MW2000 would be credited to my account. I shipped the toaster to you, and you notified me on September 15 of its receipt. Today, I received a credit card statement charging me both the price and the shipping and handling charges.

I have used your company's products in the past and have been very happy with their quality. I regret to say, however, that your after-sales service leaves much to be desired. I would be very grateful if you could credit my account with the full amount owed to me as soon as possible.

Sincerely,

Edgar Mycroft
Edgar Mycroft

Mr. Edgar Mycroft
148 Magnolia Lane
Coolangatta, QLD 4225

October 25

Dear Mr. Mycroft,

Thank you very much for your letter concerning the problems with your purchase of the MW2000 and the refund. Let me first of all apologize for the oversight that has led to the delay in crediting your account. I would like to assure you that this case is an exception as we always try to fulfill our promises to our valued customers.

I have personally instructed one of our staff members to take the necessary action to have your account credited in full amount. Furthermore, in order to make up for our mistake, I would like to offer you a 20-percent discount on any one of our products that you buy within this year.

Once again, please accept my sincere apology for the inconvenience you have suffered. We value our regular customers, and would like to do all we can to keep them happy with the quality of both our products and our service.

Sincerely,

Kylie Trevor
Customer Service Manager

191. Why did the customer experience a problem?
    (A) The company was careless.
    (B) There was a computer error.
    (C) His letter did not reach the company.
    (D) His credit card company made an error.

192. What did the customer expect the company to do?
    (A) Replace the defective product.
    (B) Send him a check.
    (C) Refund all of his costs.
    (D) Give him a discount on future purchases.

193. What did the customer do after finding the product did not work properly?
    (A) He threw it away.
    (B) He returned it to the manufacturer.
    (C) He tried to repair it by himself.
    (D) He called on the manufacturer.

194. What action did Kylie Trevor take in response to the customer's letter?
    (A) She called the customer's credit card company.
    (B) She sent the customer a new product at a lower cost.
    (C) She told one of her staff to deal with the problem.
    (D) She offered the customer a discount on all his future purchases.

195. What will be included in the refund from the company?
    (A) The costs of merchandise, handling and shipping
    (B) The cost of merchandise minus handling and shipping charges
    (C) The cost of merchandise minus 20%
    (D) The cost of merchandise plus 20%

➡ *GO ON TO THE NEXT PAGE.*

Pre Test

Half Test 1

Half Test 2

Full Test

Questions 196-200 refer to the following want ad and letter.

Wanted GERMAN-SPEAKING PERSONAL ASSISTANT
by a major global business

To work with senior executive for a support and office management role in establishing a new location in Chicago.

Salary around $40,000   Work place: Central Chicago
Based in central Chicago, this new role will support two German business development executives in the oil and gas industry. The job will focus on organizing itineraries, dealing with correspondence and arranging international travel. Ideal candidates will be highly organized and experienced administrators with strengths in audio typing who are fluent in spoken and written German. Above all, they will have the interpersonal skills to work effectively with senior executives. Please send a resume and cover letter to Frances O'Hara, Davies & Charles Co., Suite 4, Rialto Plaza, Chicago IL 60608.

Ms. Frances O'Hara
Davies & Charles Co.
Suite 4, 47 Rialto Plaza
Chicago IL 60608

Dear Ms. O'Hara.
I am writing in response to the advertisement for the position of German-speaking personal assistant. I am very interested in the position and believe I am well-qualified for it. I am completely bilingual in English and German. In fact my father is German, and I spent my childhood in Germany. When I was 14, my family moved to the United States, where I went to high school and university. I also speak French and Italian at a high level.

As you will see from my résumé, I have spent the last five years working in administrative positions. Although this experience has been mainly in the financial services industry, I feel it is nevertheless relevant as I spent two years helping a German bank set up its first office in the U.S.

I believe I could be a great asset to your organization, and I look forward very much to the opportunity of an interview.

Sincerely yours,

Margarete Hirsch

Margarete Hirsch

196. Where will the job be based?
    (A) Germany
    (B) Italy
    (C) The United States
    (D) France

197. What kind of person should apply for this position?
    (A) Someone who is good at human relations
    (B) Someone who is willing to learn
    (C) Someone who can type well
    (D) Someone who is quick in decision making

198. Why does Margarete Hirsh think she is well-qualified for the job?
    (A) Because of her experience in the oil and gas industry
    (B) Because of her command of English
    (C) Because of her banking experience in Germany
    (D) Because of her command of German

199. How did Margarete Hirsh learn German?
    (A) She studied it at university.
    (B) She lived in Germany as a child.
    (C) She worked in a German company.
    (D) She traveled to Germany for a few times.

200. In the want ad, the word "interpersonal" in line 6, is closest in meaning to
    (A) International
    (B) Person-to-person
    (C) Tactful and kind
    (D) Clever and thoughtful

Stop! This is the end of the test. If you finish before time is called, you may go back to Parts 5, 6, and 7 and check your work.

Pre Test Answer Sheet

Name

LISTENING SECTION

Part 1

No.	ANSWER A B C D
1	Ⓐ Ⓑ Ⓒ Ⓓ
2	Ⓐ Ⓑ Ⓒ Ⓓ
3	Ⓐ Ⓑ Ⓒ Ⓓ
4	Ⓐ Ⓑ Ⓒ Ⓓ
5	Ⓐ Ⓑ Ⓒ Ⓓ
6	Ⓐ Ⓑ Ⓒ Ⓓ
7	Ⓐ Ⓑ Ⓒ Ⓓ
8	Ⓐ Ⓑ Ⓒ Ⓓ
9	Ⓐ Ⓑ Ⓒ Ⓓ
10	Ⓐ Ⓑ Ⓒ Ⓓ

Part 2

No.	ANSWER A B C D
11	Ⓐ Ⓑ Ⓒ Ⓓ
12	Ⓐ Ⓑ Ⓒ Ⓓ
13	Ⓐ Ⓑ Ⓒ Ⓓ
14	Ⓐ Ⓑ Ⓒ Ⓓ
15	Ⓐ Ⓑ Ⓒ Ⓓ
16	Ⓐ Ⓑ Ⓒ Ⓓ
17	Ⓐ Ⓑ Ⓒ Ⓓ
18	Ⓐ Ⓑ Ⓒ Ⓓ
19	Ⓐ Ⓑ Ⓒ Ⓓ
20	Ⓐ Ⓑ Ⓒ Ⓓ

Part 3

No.	ANSWER A B C D	No.	ANSWER A B C D
21	Ⓐ Ⓑ Ⓒ Ⓓ	31	Ⓐ Ⓑ Ⓒ Ⓓ
22	Ⓐ Ⓑ Ⓒ Ⓓ	32	Ⓐ Ⓑ Ⓒ Ⓓ
23	Ⓐ Ⓑ Ⓒ Ⓓ	33	Ⓐ Ⓑ Ⓒ Ⓓ
24	Ⓐ Ⓑ Ⓒ Ⓓ	34	Ⓐ Ⓑ Ⓒ Ⓓ
25	Ⓐ Ⓑ Ⓒ Ⓓ	35	Ⓐ Ⓑ Ⓒ Ⓓ
26	Ⓐ Ⓑ Ⓒ Ⓓ	36	Ⓐ Ⓑ Ⓒ Ⓓ
27	Ⓐ Ⓑ Ⓒ Ⓓ	37	Ⓐ Ⓑ Ⓒ Ⓓ
28	Ⓐ Ⓑ Ⓒ Ⓓ	38	Ⓐ Ⓑ Ⓒ Ⓓ
29	Ⓐ Ⓑ Ⓒ Ⓓ	39	Ⓐ Ⓑ Ⓒ Ⓓ
30	Ⓐ Ⓑ Ⓒ Ⓓ	40	Ⓐ Ⓑ Ⓒ Ⓓ

Part 4

No.	ANSWER A B C D
41	Ⓐ Ⓑ Ⓒ Ⓓ
42	Ⓐ Ⓑ Ⓒ Ⓓ
43	Ⓐ Ⓑ Ⓒ Ⓓ
44	Ⓐ Ⓑ Ⓒ Ⓓ
45	Ⓐ Ⓑ Ⓒ Ⓓ
46	Ⓐ Ⓑ Ⓒ Ⓓ
47	Ⓐ Ⓑ Ⓒ Ⓓ
48	Ⓐ Ⓑ Ⓒ Ⓓ
49	Ⓐ Ⓑ Ⓒ Ⓓ
50	Ⓐ Ⓑ Ⓒ Ⓓ

READING SECTION

Part 5

No.	ANSWER A B C D	No.	ANSWER A B C D
51	Ⓐ Ⓑ Ⓒ Ⓓ	61	Ⓐ Ⓑ Ⓒ Ⓓ
52	Ⓐ Ⓑ Ⓒ Ⓓ	62	Ⓐ Ⓑ Ⓒ Ⓓ
53	Ⓐ Ⓑ Ⓒ Ⓓ	63	Ⓐ Ⓑ Ⓒ Ⓓ
54	Ⓐ Ⓑ Ⓒ Ⓓ	64	Ⓐ Ⓑ Ⓒ Ⓓ
55	Ⓐ Ⓑ Ⓒ Ⓓ	65	Ⓐ Ⓑ Ⓒ Ⓓ
56	Ⓐ Ⓑ Ⓒ Ⓓ	66	Ⓐ Ⓑ Ⓒ Ⓓ
57	Ⓐ Ⓑ Ⓒ Ⓓ	67	Ⓐ Ⓑ Ⓒ Ⓓ
58	Ⓐ Ⓑ Ⓒ Ⓓ	68	Ⓐ Ⓑ Ⓒ Ⓓ
59	Ⓐ Ⓑ Ⓒ Ⓓ	69	Ⓐ Ⓑ Ⓒ Ⓓ
60	Ⓐ Ⓑ Ⓒ Ⓓ	70	Ⓐ Ⓑ Ⓒ Ⓓ

Part 6

No.	ANSWER A B C D
71	Ⓐ Ⓑ Ⓒ Ⓓ
72	Ⓐ Ⓑ Ⓒ Ⓓ
73	Ⓐ Ⓑ Ⓒ Ⓓ
74	Ⓐ Ⓑ Ⓒ Ⓓ
75	Ⓐ Ⓑ Ⓒ Ⓓ
76	Ⓐ Ⓑ Ⓒ Ⓓ
77	Ⓐ Ⓑ Ⓒ Ⓓ
78	Ⓐ Ⓑ Ⓒ Ⓓ
79	Ⓐ Ⓑ Ⓒ Ⓓ
80	Ⓐ Ⓑ Ⓒ Ⓓ

Part 7

No.	ANSWER A B C D	No.	ANSWER A B C D
81	Ⓐ Ⓑ Ⓒ Ⓓ	91	Ⓐ Ⓑ Ⓒ Ⓓ
82	Ⓐ Ⓑ Ⓒ Ⓓ	92	Ⓐ Ⓑ Ⓒ Ⓓ
83	Ⓐ Ⓑ Ⓒ Ⓓ	93	Ⓐ Ⓑ Ⓒ Ⓓ
84	Ⓐ Ⓑ Ⓒ Ⓓ	94	Ⓐ Ⓑ Ⓒ Ⓓ
85	Ⓐ Ⓑ Ⓒ Ⓓ	95	Ⓐ Ⓑ Ⓒ Ⓓ
86	Ⓐ Ⓑ Ⓒ Ⓓ	96	Ⓐ Ⓑ Ⓒ Ⓓ
87	Ⓐ Ⓑ Ⓒ Ⓓ	97	Ⓐ Ⓑ Ⓒ Ⓓ
88	Ⓐ Ⓑ Ⓒ Ⓓ	98	Ⓐ Ⓑ Ⓒ Ⓓ
89	Ⓐ Ⓑ Ⓒ Ⓓ	99	Ⓐ Ⓑ Ⓒ Ⓓ
90	Ⓐ Ⓑ Ⓒ Ⓓ	100	Ⓐ Ⓑ Ⓒ Ⓓ

Pre Test Answer Sheet

Name

LISTENING SECTION

Part 1

No.	ANSWER A B C D
1	A B C D
2	A B C D
3	A B C D
4	A B C D
5	A B C D
6	A B C D
7	A B C D
8	A B C D
9	A B C D
10	A B C D

Part 2

No.	ANSWER A B C D
11	A B C D
12	A B C D
13	A B C D
14	A B C D
15	A B C D
16	A B C D
17	A B C D
18	A B C D
19	A B C D
20	A B C D

Part 3

No.	ANSWER A B C D
21	A B C D
22	A B C D
23	A B C D
24	A B C D
25	A B C D
26	A B C D
27	A B C D
28	A B C D
29	A B C D
30	A B C D

No.	ANSWER A B C D
31	A B C D
32	A B C D
33	A B C D
34	A B C D
35	A B C D
36	A B C D
37	A B C D
38	A B C D
39	A B C D
40	A B C D

Part 4

No.	ANSWER A B C D
41	A B C D
42	A B C D
43	A B C D
44	A B C D
45	A B C D
46	A B C D
47	A B C D
48	A B C D
49	A B C D
50	A B C D

READING SECTION

Part 5

No.	ANSWER A B C D
51	A B C D
52	A B C D
53	A B C D
54	A B C D
55	A B C D
56	A B C D
57	A B C D
58	A B C D
59	A B C D
60	A B C D

No.	ANSWER A B C D
61	A B C D
62	A B C D
63	A B C D
64	A B C D
65	A B C D
66	A B C D
67	A B C D
68	A B C D
69	A B C D
70	A B C D

Part 6

No.	ANSWER A B C D
71	A B C D
72	A B C D
73	A B C D
74	A B C D
75	A B C D
76	A B C D
77	A B C D
78	A B C D
79	A B C D
80	A B C D

Part 7

No.	ANSWER A B C D
81	A B C D
82	A B C D
83	A B C D
84	A B C D
85	A B C D
86	A B C D
87	A B C D
88	A B C D
89	A B C D
90	A B C D

No.	ANSWER A B C D
91	A B C D
92	A B C D
93	A B C D
94	A B C D
95	A B C D
96	A B C D
97	A B C D
98	A B C D
99	A B C D
100	A B C D

Half Test 1 Answer Sheet

Name

LISTENING SECTION

Part 1

No.	ANSWER A B C D
1	A B C D
2	A B C D
3	A B C D
4	A B C D
5	A B C D
6	A B C D
7	A B C D
8	A B C D
9	A B C D
10	A B C D

Part 2

No.	ANSWER A B C D
11	A B C D
12	A B C D
13	A B C D
14	A B C D
15	A B C D
16	A B C D
17	A B C D
18	A B C D
19	A B C D
20	A B C D

Part 3

No.	ANSWER A B C D	No.	ANSWER A B C D
21	A B C D	31	A B C D
22	A B C D	32	A B C D
23	A B C D	33	A B C D
24	A B C D	34	A B C D
25	A B C D	35	A B C D
26	A B C D	36	A B C D
27	A B C D	37	A B C D
28	A B C D	38	A B C D
29	A B C D	39	A B C D
30	A B C D	40	A B C D

Part 4

No.	ANSWER A B C D
41	A B C D
42	A B C D
43	A B C D
44	A B C D
45	A B C D
46	A B C D
47	A B C D
48	A B C D
49	A B C D
50	A B C D

READING SECTION

Part 5

No.	ANSWER A B C D	No.	ANSWER A B C D
51	A B C D	61	A B C D
52	A B C D	62	A B C D
53	A B C D	63	A B C D
54	A B C D	64	A B C D
55	A B C D	65	A B C D
56	A B C D	66	A B C D
57	A B C D	67	A B C D
58	A B C D	68	A B C D
59	A B C D	69	A B C D
60	A B C D	70	A B C D

Part 6

No.	ANSWER A B C D
71	A B C D
72	A B C D
73	A B C D
74	A B C D
75	A B C D
76	A B C D
77	A B C D
78	A B C D
79	A B C D
80	A B C D

Part 7

No.	ANSWER A B C D	No.	ANSWER A B C D
81	A B C D	91	A B C D
82	A B C D	92	A B C D
83	A B C D	93	A B C D
84	A B C D	94	A B C D
85	A B C D	95	A B C D
86	A B C D	96	A B C D
87	A B C D	97	A B C D
88	A B C D	98	A B C D
89	A B C D	99	A B C D
90	A B C D	100	A B C D

Half Test 1 Answer Sheet

Name

LISTENING SECTION

Part 1

No.	ANSWER A B C D
1	A B C D
2	A B C D
3	A B C D
4	A B C D
5	A B C D
6	A B C D
7	A B C D
8	A B C D
9	A B C D
10	A B C D

Part 2

No.	ANSWER A B C D
11	A B C D
12	A B C D
13	A B C D
14	A B C D
15	A B C D
16	A B C D
17	A B C D
18	A B C D
19	A B C D
20	A B C D

Part 3

No.	ANSWER A B C D	No.	ANSWER A B C D
21	A B C D	31	A B C D
22	A B C D	32	A B C D
23	A B C D	33	A B C D
24	A B C D	34	A B C D
25	A B C D	35	A B C D
26	A B C D	36	A B C D
27	A B C D	37	A B C D
28	A B C D	38	A B C D
29	A B C D	39	A B C D
30	A B C D	40	A B C D

Part 4

No.	ANSWER A B C D
41	A B C D
42	A B C D
43	A B C D
44	A B C D
45	A B C D
46	A B C D
47	A B C D
48	A B C D
49	A B C D
50	A B C D

READING SECTION

Part 5

No.	ANSWER A B C D	No.	ANSWER A B C D
51	A B C D	61	A B C D
52	A B C D	62	A B C D
53	A B C D	63	A B C D
54	A B C D	64	A B C D
55	A B C D	65	A B C D
56	A B C D	66	A B C D
57	A B C D	67	A B C D
58	A B C D	68	A B C D
59	A B C D	69	A B C D
60	A B C D	70	A B C D

Part 6

No.	ANSWER A B C D
71	A B C D
72	A B C D
73	A B C D
74	A B C D
75	A B C D
76	A B C D
77	A B C D
78	A B C D
79	A B C D
80	A B C D

Part 7

No.	ANSWER A B C D	No.	ANSWER A B C D
81	A B C D	91	A B C D
82	A B C D	92	A B C D
83	A B C D	93	A B C D
84	A B C D	94	A B C D
85	A B C D	95	A B C D
86	A B C D	96	A B C D
87	A B C D	97	A B C D
88	A B C D	98	A B C D
89	A B C D	99	A B C D
90	A B C D	100	A B C D

Half Test 2 Answer Sheet

Name

LISTENING SECTION

Part 1

No.	ANSWER A B C D
1	Ⓐ Ⓑ Ⓒ Ⓓ
2	Ⓐ Ⓑ Ⓒ Ⓓ
3	Ⓐ Ⓑ Ⓒ Ⓓ
4	Ⓐ Ⓑ Ⓒ Ⓓ
5	Ⓐ Ⓑ Ⓒ Ⓓ
6	Ⓐ Ⓑ Ⓒ Ⓓ
7	Ⓐ Ⓑ Ⓒ Ⓓ
8	Ⓐ Ⓑ Ⓒ Ⓓ
9	Ⓐ Ⓑ Ⓒ Ⓓ
10	Ⓐ Ⓑ Ⓒ Ⓓ

Part 2

No.	ANSWER A B C D
11	Ⓐ Ⓑ Ⓒ Ⓓ
12	Ⓐ Ⓑ Ⓒ Ⓓ
13	Ⓐ Ⓑ Ⓒ Ⓓ
14	Ⓐ Ⓑ Ⓒ Ⓓ
15	Ⓐ Ⓑ Ⓒ Ⓓ
16	Ⓐ Ⓑ Ⓒ Ⓓ
17	Ⓐ Ⓑ Ⓒ Ⓓ
18	Ⓐ Ⓑ Ⓒ Ⓓ
19	Ⓐ Ⓑ Ⓒ Ⓓ
20	Ⓐ Ⓑ Ⓒ Ⓓ

Part 3

No.	ANSWER A B C D
21	Ⓐ Ⓑ Ⓒ Ⓓ
22	Ⓐ Ⓑ Ⓒ Ⓓ
23	Ⓐ Ⓑ Ⓒ Ⓓ
24	Ⓐ Ⓑ Ⓒ Ⓓ
25	Ⓐ Ⓑ Ⓒ Ⓓ
26	Ⓐ Ⓑ Ⓒ Ⓓ
27	Ⓐ Ⓑ Ⓒ Ⓓ
28	Ⓐ Ⓑ Ⓒ Ⓓ
29	Ⓐ Ⓑ Ⓒ Ⓓ
30	Ⓐ Ⓑ Ⓒ Ⓓ

No.	ANSWER A B C D
31	Ⓐ Ⓑ Ⓒ Ⓓ
32	Ⓐ Ⓑ Ⓒ Ⓓ
33	Ⓐ Ⓑ Ⓒ Ⓓ
34	Ⓐ Ⓑ Ⓒ Ⓓ
35	Ⓐ Ⓑ Ⓒ Ⓓ
36	Ⓐ Ⓑ Ⓒ Ⓓ
37	Ⓐ Ⓑ Ⓒ Ⓓ
38	Ⓐ Ⓑ Ⓒ Ⓓ
39	Ⓐ Ⓑ Ⓒ Ⓓ
40	Ⓐ Ⓑ Ⓒ Ⓓ

Part 4

No.	ANSWER A B C D
41	Ⓐ Ⓑ Ⓒ Ⓓ
42	Ⓐ Ⓑ Ⓒ Ⓓ
43	Ⓐ Ⓑ Ⓒ Ⓓ
44	Ⓐ Ⓑ Ⓒ Ⓓ
45	Ⓐ Ⓑ Ⓒ Ⓓ
46	Ⓐ Ⓑ Ⓒ Ⓓ
47	Ⓐ Ⓑ Ⓒ Ⓓ
48	Ⓐ Ⓑ Ⓒ Ⓓ
49	Ⓐ Ⓑ Ⓒ Ⓓ
50	Ⓐ Ⓑ Ⓒ Ⓓ

READING SECTION

Part 5

No.	ANSWER A B C D
51	Ⓐ Ⓑ Ⓒ Ⓓ
52	Ⓐ Ⓑ Ⓒ Ⓓ
53	Ⓐ Ⓑ Ⓒ Ⓓ
54	Ⓐ Ⓑ Ⓒ Ⓓ
55	Ⓐ Ⓑ Ⓒ Ⓓ
56	Ⓐ Ⓑ Ⓒ Ⓓ
57	Ⓐ Ⓑ Ⓒ Ⓓ
58	Ⓐ Ⓑ Ⓒ Ⓓ
59	Ⓐ Ⓑ Ⓒ Ⓓ
60	Ⓐ Ⓑ Ⓒ Ⓓ

No.	ANSWER A B C D
61	Ⓐ Ⓑ Ⓒ Ⓓ
62	Ⓐ Ⓑ Ⓒ Ⓓ
63	Ⓐ Ⓑ Ⓒ Ⓓ
64	Ⓐ Ⓑ Ⓒ Ⓓ
65	Ⓐ Ⓑ Ⓒ Ⓓ
66	Ⓐ Ⓑ Ⓒ Ⓓ
67	Ⓐ Ⓑ Ⓒ Ⓓ
68	Ⓐ Ⓑ Ⓒ Ⓓ
69	Ⓐ Ⓑ Ⓒ Ⓓ
70	Ⓐ Ⓑ Ⓒ Ⓓ

Part 6

No.	ANSWER A B C D
71	Ⓐ Ⓑ Ⓒ Ⓓ
72	Ⓐ Ⓑ Ⓒ Ⓓ
73	Ⓐ Ⓑ Ⓒ Ⓓ
74	Ⓐ Ⓑ Ⓒ Ⓓ
75	Ⓐ Ⓑ Ⓒ Ⓓ
76	Ⓐ Ⓑ Ⓒ Ⓓ
77	Ⓐ Ⓑ Ⓒ Ⓓ
78	Ⓐ Ⓑ Ⓒ Ⓓ
79	Ⓐ Ⓑ Ⓒ Ⓓ
80	Ⓐ Ⓑ Ⓒ Ⓓ

Part 7

No.	ANSWER A B C D
81	Ⓐ Ⓑ Ⓒ Ⓓ
82	Ⓐ Ⓑ Ⓒ Ⓓ
83	Ⓐ Ⓑ Ⓒ Ⓓ
84	Ⓐ Ⓑ Ⓒ Ⓓ
85	Ⓐ Ⓑ Ⓒ Ⓓ
86	Ⓐ Ⓑ Ⓒ Ⓓ
87	Ⓐ Ⓑ Ⓒ Ⓓ
88	Ⓐ Ⓑ Ⓒ Ⓓ
89	Ⓐ Ⓑ Ⓒ Ⓓ
90	Ⓐ Ⓑ Ⓒ Ⓓ

No.	ANSWER A B C D
91	Ⓐ Ⓑ Ⓒ Ⓓ
92	Ⓐ Ⓑ Ⓒ Ⓓ
93	Ⓐ Ⓑ Ⓒ Ⓓ
94	Ⓐ Ⓑ Ⓒ Ⓓ
95	Ⓐ Ⓑ Ⓒ Ⓓ
96	Ⓐ Ⓑ Ⓒ Ⓓ
97	Ⓐ Ⓑ Ⓒ Ⓓ
98	Ⓐ Ⓑ Ⓒ Ⓓ
99	Ⓐ Ⓑ Ⓒ Ⓓ
100	Ⓐ Ⓑ Ⓒ Ⓓ

Half Test 2 Answer Sheet

Name

LISTENING SECTION

Part 1

No.	ANSWER A B C D
1	Ⓐ Ⓑ Ⓒ Ⓓ
2	Ⓐ Ⓑ Ⓒ Ⓓ
3	Ⓐ Ⓑ Ⓒ Ⓓ
4	Ⓐ Ⓑ Ⓒ Ⓓ
5	Ⓐ Ⓑ Ⓒ Ⓓ
6	Ⓐ Ⓑ Ⓒ Ⓓ
7	Ⓐ Ⓑ Ⓒ Ⓓ
8	Ⓐ Ⓑ Ⓒ Ⓓ
9	Ⓐ Ⓑ Ⓒ Ⓓ
10	Ⓐ Ⓑ Ⓒ Ⓓ

Part 2

No.	ANSWER A B C D
11	Ⓐ Ⓑ Ⓒ Ⓓ
12	Ⓐ Ⓑ Ⓒ Ⓓ
13	Ⓐ Ⓑ Ⓒ Ⓓ
14	Ⓐ Ⓑ Ⓒ Ⓓ
15	Ⓐ Ⓑ Ⓒ Ⓓ
16	Ⓐ Ⓑ Ⓒ Ⓓ
17	Ⓐ Ⓑ Ⓒ Ⓓ
18	Ⓐ Ⓑ Ⓒ Ⓓ
19	Ⓐ Ⓑ Ⓒ Ⓓ
20	Ⓐ Ⓑ Ⓒ Ⓓ

Part 3

No.	ANSWER A B C D
21	Ⓐ Ⓑ Ⓒ Ⓓ
22	Ⓐ Ⓑ Ⓒ Ⓓ
23	Ⓐ Ⓑ Ⓒ Ⓓ
24	Ⓐ Ⓑ Ⓒ Ⓓ
25	Ⓐ Ⓑ Ⓒ Ⓓ
26	Ⓐ Ⓑ Ⓒ Ⓓ
27	Ⓐ Ⓑ Ⓒ Ⓓ
28	Ⓐ Ⓑ Ⓒ Ⓓ
29	Ⓐ Ⓑ Ⓒ Ⓓ
30	Ⓐ Ⓑ Ⓒ Ⓓ

No.	ANSWER A B C D
31	Ⓐ Ⓑ Ⓒ Ⓓ
32	Ⓐ Ⓑ Ⓒ Ⓓ
33	Ⓐ Ⓑ Ⓒ Ⓓ
34	Ⓐ Ⓑ Ⓒ Ⓓ
35	Ⓐ Ⓑ Ⓒ Ⓓ
36	Ⓐ Ⓑ Ⓒ Ⓓ
37	Ⓐ Ⓑ Ⓒ Ⓓ
38	Ⓐ Ⓑ Ⓒ Ⓓ
39	Ⓐ Ⓑ Ⓒ Ⓓ
40	Ⓐ Ⓑ Ⓒ Ⓓ

Part 4

No.	ANSWER A B C D
41	Ⓐ Ⓑ Ⓒ Ⓓ
42	Ⓐ Ⓑ Ⓒ Ⓓ
43	Ⓐ Ⓑ Ⓒ Ⓓ
44	Ⓐ Ⓑ Ⓒ Ⓓ
45	Ⓐ Ⓑ Ⓒ Ⓓ
46	Ⓐ Ⓑ Ⓒ Ⓓ
47	Ⓐ Ⓑ Ⓒ Ⓓ
48	Ⓐ Ⓑ Ⓒ Ⓓ
49	Ⓐ Ⓑ Ⓒ Ⓓ
50	Ⓐ Ⓑ Ⓒ Ⓓ

READING SECTION

Part 5

No.	ANSWER A B C D
51	Ⓐ Ⓑ Ⓒ Ⓓ
52	Ⓐ Ⓑ Ⓒ Ⓓ
53	Ⓐ Ⓑ Ⓒ Ⓓ
54	Ⓐ Ⓑ Ⓒ Ⓓ
55	Ⓐ Ⓑ Ⓒ Ⓓ
56	Ⓐ Ⓑ Ⓒ Ⓓ
57	Ⓐ Ⓑ Ⓒ Ⓓ
58	Ⓐ Ⓑ Ⓒ Ⓓ
59	Ⓐ Ⓑ Ⓒ Ⓓ
60	Ⓐ Ⓑ Ⓒ Ⓓ

No.	ANSWER A B C D
61	Ⓐ Ⓑ Ⓒ Ⓓ
62	Ⓐ Ⓑ Ⓒ Ⓓ
63	Ⓐ Ⓑ Ⓒ Ⓓ
64	Ⓐ Ⓑ Ⓒ Ⓓ
65	Ⓐ Ⓑ Ⓒ Ⓓ
66	Ⓐ Ⓑ Ⓒ Ⓓ
67	Ⓐ Ⓑ Ⓒ Ⓓ
68	Ⓐ Ⓑ Ⓒ Ⓓ
69	Ⓐ Ⓑ Ⓒ Ⓓ
70	Ⓐ Ⓑ Ⓒ Ⓓ

Part 6

No.	ANSWER A B C D
71	Ⓐ Ⓑ Ⓒ Ⓓ
72	Ⓐ Ⓑ Ⓒ Ⓓ
73	Ⓐ Ⓑ Ⓒ Ⓓ
74	Ⓐ Ⓑ Ⓒ Ⓓ
75	Ⓐ Ⓑ Ⓒ Ⓓ
76	Ⓐ Ⓑ Ⓒ Ⓓ
77	Ⓐ Ⓑ Ⓒ Ⓓ
78	Ⓐ Ⓑ Ⓒ Ⓓ
79	Ⓐ Ⓑ Ⓒ Ⓓ
80	Ⓐ Ⓑ Ⓒ Ⓓ

Part 7

No.	ANSWER A B C D
81	Ⓐ Ⓑ Ⓒ Ⓓ
82	Ⓐ Ⓑ Ⓒ Ⓓ
83	Ⓐ Ⓑ Ⓒ Ⓓ
84	Ⓐ Ⓑ Ⓒ Ⓓ
85	Ⓐ Ⓑ Ⓒ Ⓓ
86	Ⓐ Ⓑ Ⓒ Ⓓ
87	Ⓐ Ⓑ Ⓒ Ⓓ
88	Ⓐ Ⓑ Ⓒ Ⓓ
89	Ⓐ Ⓑ Ⓒ Ⓓ
90	Ⓐ Ⓑ Ⓒ Ⓓ

No.	ANSWER A B C D
91	Ⓐ Ⓑ Ⓒ Ⓓ
92	Ⓐ Ⓑ Ⓒ Ⓓ
93	Ⓐ Ⓑ Ⓒ Ⓓ
94	Ⓐ Ⓑ Ⓒ Ⓓ
95	Ⓐ Ⓑ Ⓒ Ⓓ
96	Ⓐ Ⓑ Ⓒ Ⓓ
97	Ⓐ Ⓑ Ⓒ Ⓓ
98	Ⓐ Ⓑ Ⓒ Ⓓ
99	Ⓐ Ⓑ Ⓒ Ⓓ
100	Ⓐ Ⓑ Ⓒ Ⓓ

Full Test Answer Sheet

Name

LISTENING SECTION

Part 1

No.	ANSWER A B C D
1	A B C D
2	A B C D
3	A B C D
4	A B C D
5	A B C D
6	A B C D
7	A B C D
8	A B C D
9	A B C D
10	A B C D

Part 2

No.	ANSWER A B C D
11	A B C D
12	A B C D
13	A B C D
14	A B C D
15	A B C D
16	A B C D
17	A B C D
18	A B C D
19	A B C D
20	A B C D
21	A B C D
22	A B C D
23	A B C D
24	A B C D
25	A B C D
26	A B C D
27	A B C D
28	A B C D
29	A B C D
30	A B C D

Part 3

No.	ANSWER A B C D
31	A B C D
32	A B C D
33	A B C D
34	A B C D
35	A B C D
36	A B C D
37	A B C D
38	A B C D
39	A B C D
40	A B C D
41	A B C D
42	A B C D
43	A B C D
44	A B C D
45	A B C D
46	A B C D
47	A B C D
48	A B C D
49	A B C D
50	A B C D
51	A B C D
52	A B C D
53	A B C D
54	A B C D
55	A B C D
56	A B C D
57	A B C D
58	A B C D
59	A B C D
60	A B C D
61	A B C D
62	A B C D
63	A B C D
64	A B C D
65	A B C D
66	A B C D
67	A B C D
68	A B C D
69	A B C D
70	A B C D

Part 4

No.	ANSWER A B C D
71	A B C D
72	A B C D
73	A B C D
74	A B C D
75	A B C D
76	A B C D
77	A B C D
78	A B C D
79	A B C D
80	A B C D
81	A B C D
82	A B C D
83	A B C D
84	A B C D
85	A B C D
86	A B C D
87	A B C D
88	A B C D
89	A B C D
90	A B C D
91	A B C D
92	A B C D
93	A B C D
94	A B C D
95	A B C D
96	A B C D
97	A B C D
98	A B C D
99	A B C D
100	A B C D

READING SECTION

Part 5

No.	ANSWER A B C D
101	A B C D
102	A B C D
103	A B C D
104	A B C D
105	A B C D
106	A B C D
107	A B C D
108	A B C D
109	A B C D
110	A B C D
111	A B C D
112	A B C D
113	A B C D
114	A B C D
115	A B C D
116	A B C D
117	A B C D
118	A B C D
119	A B C D
120	A B C D
121	A B C D
122	A B C D
123	A B C D
124	A B C D
125	A B C D
126	A B C D
127	A B C D
128	A B C D
129	A B C D
130	A B C D
131	A B C D
132	A B C D
133	A B C D
134	A B C D
135	A B C D
136	A B C D
137	A B C D
138	A B C D
139	A B C D
140	A B C D

Part 6

No.	ANSWER A B C D
141	A B C D
142	A B C D
143	A B C D
144	A B C D
145	A B C D
146	A B C D
147	A B C D
148	A B C D
149	A B C D
150	A B C D
151	A B C D
152	A B C D
153	A B C D
154	A B C D
155	A B C D
156	A B C D
157	A B C D
158	A B C D
159	A B C D
160	A B C D

Part 7

No.	ANSWER A B C D
161	A B C D
162	A B C D
163	A B C D
164	A B C D
165	A B C D
166	A B C D
167	A B C D
168	A B C D
169	A B C D
170	A B C D
171	A B C D
172	A B C D
173	A B C D
174	A B C D
175	A B C D
176	A B C D
177	A B C D
178	A B C D
179	A B C D
180	A B C D
181	A B C D
182	A B C D
183	A B C D
184	A B C D
185	A B C D
186	A B C D
187	A B C D
188	A B C D
189	A B C D
190	A B C D
191	A B C D
192	A B C D
193	A B C D
194	A B C D
195	A B C D
196	A B C D
197	A B C D
198	A B C D
199	A B C D
200	A B C D

Full Test Answer Sheet

Name	

LISTENING SECTION

Part 1		Part 2						Part 3						Part 4					
No.	ANSWER A B C D	No.	ANSWER A B C D	No.	ANSWER A B C D	No.	ANSWER A B C D	No.	ANSWER A B C D	No.	ANSWER A B C D	No.	ANSWER A B C D	No.	ANSWER A B C D	No.	ANSWER A B C D	No.	ANSWER A B C D
1	A B C D	11	A B C D	21	A B C D	31	A B C D	41	A B C D	51	A B C D	61	A B C D	71	A B C D	81	A B C D	91	A B C D
2	A B C D	12	A B C D	22	A B C D	32	A B C D	42	A B C D	52	A B C D	62	A B C D	72	A B C D	82	A B C D	92	A B C D
3	A B C D	13	A B C D	23	A B C D	33	A B C D	43	A B C D	53	A B C D	63	A B C D	73	A B C D	83	A B C D	93	A B C D
4	A B C D	14	A B C D	24	A B C D	34	A B C D	44	A B C D	54	A B C D	64	A B C D	74	A B C D	84	A B C D	94	A B C D
5	A B C D	15	A B C D	25	A B C D	35	A B C D	45	A B C D	55	A B C D	65	A B C D	75	A B C D	85	A B C D	95	A B C D
6	A B C D	16	A B C D	26	A B C D	36	A B C D	46	A B C D	56	A B C D	66	A B C D	76	A B C D	86	A B C D	96	A B C D
7	A B C D	17	A B C D	27	A B C D	37	A B C D	47	A B C D	57	A B C D	67	A B C D	77	A B C D	87	A B C D	97	A B C D
8	A B C D	18	A B C D	28	A B C D	38	A B C D	48	A B C D	58	A B C D	68	A B C D	78	A B C D	88	A B C D	98	A B C D
9	A B C D	19	A B C D	29	A B C D	39	A B C D	49	A B C D	59	A B C D	69	A B C D	79	A B C D	89	A B C D	99	A B C D
10	A B C D	20	A B C D	30	A B C D	40	A B C D	50	A B C D	60	A B C D	70	A B C D	80	A B C D	90	A B C D	100	A B C D

READING SECTION

Part 5								Part 6				Part 7							
No.	ANSWER A B C D	No.	ANSWER A B C D	No.	ANSWER A B C D	No.	ANSWER A B C D	No.	ANSWER A B C D	No.	ANSWER A B C D	No.	ANSWER A B C D	No.	ANSWER A B C D	No.	ANSWER A B C D	No.	ANSWER A B C D
101	A B C D	111	A B C D	121	A B C D	131	A B C D	141	A B C D	151	A B C D	161	A B C D	171	A B C D	181	A B C D	191	A B C D
102	A B C D	112	A B C D	122	A B C D	132	A B C D	142	A B C D	152	A B C D	162	A B C D	172	A B C D	182	A B C D	192	A B C D
103	A B C D	113	A B C D	123	A B C D	133	A B C D	143	A B C D	153	A B C D	163	A B C D	173	A B C D	183	A B C D	193	A B C D
104	A B C D	114	A B C D	124	A B C D	134	A B C D	144	A B C D	154	A B C D	164	A B C D	174	A B C D	184	A B C D	194	A B C D
105	A B C D	115	A B C D	125	A B C D	135	A B C D	145	A B C D	155	A B C D	165	A B C D	175	A B C D	185	A B C D	195	A B C D
106	A B C D	116	A B C D	126	A B C D	136	A B C D	146	A B C D	156	A B C D	166	A B C D	176	A B C D	186	A B C D	196	A B C D
107	A B C D	117	A B C D	127	A B C D	137	A B C D	147	A B C D	157	A B C D	167	A B C D	177	A B C D	187	A B C D	197	A B C D
108	A B C D	118	A B C D	128	A B C D	138	A B C D	148	A B C D	158	A B C D	168	A B C D	178	A B C D	188	A B C D	198	A B C D
109	A B C D	119	A B C D	129	A B C D	139	A B C D	149	A B C D	159	A B C D	169	A B C D	179	A B C D	189	A B C D	199	A B C D
110	A B C D	120	A B C D	130	A B C D	140	A B C D	150	A B C D	160	A B C D	170	A B C D	180	A B C D	190	A B C D	200	A B C D